# MASQUERADE

By

SONDRA LUGER

**Gotham Books**

30 N Gould St.
Ste. 20820, Sheridan, WY 82801
https://gothambooksinc.com/

Phone: 1 (307) 464-7800

© 2023 *Sondra Luger*. All rights reserved.

No part of this book may be reproduced, stored in a retrieval system, or transmitted by any means without the written permission of the author.

Published by Gotham Books (November 17, 2023)

ISBN: 979-8-88775-540-3 (H)
ISBN: 979-8-88775-538-0 (P)
ISBN: 979-8-88775-539-7 (E)

Because of the dynamic nature of the Internet, any web addresses or links contained in this book may have changed since publication and may no longer be valid.

The views expressed in this work are solely those of the author and do not necessarily reflect the views of the publisher, and the publisher hereby disclaims any responsibility for them.

# TABLE OF CONTENTS

| | |
|---|---:|
| CHAPTER ONE | 1 |
| CHAPTER TWO | 8 |
| CHAPTER THREE | 13 |
| CHAPTER FOUR | 18 |
| CHAPTER FIVE | 22 |
| CHAPTER SIX | 30 |
| CHAPTER SEVEN | 35 |
| CHAPTER EIGHT | 42 |
| CHAPTER NINE | 48 |
| CHAPTER TEN | 57 |
| CHAPTER ELEVEN | 61 |
| CHAPTER TWELVE | 71 |
| CHAPTER THIRTEEN | 80 |
| CHAPTER FOURTEEN | 87 |
| CHAPTER FIFTEEN | 99 |
| CHAPTER SIXTEEN | 107 |
| CHAPTER SEVENTEEN | 114 |
| CHAPTER EIGHTEEN | 126 |
| CHAPTER NINETEEN | 135 |
| CHAPTER TWENTY | 139 |
| CHAPTER TWENTY-ONE | 143 |
| CHAPTER TWENTY-TWO | 148 |
| CHAPTER TWENTY-THREE | 156 |
| CHAPTER TWENTY-FOUR | 165 |
| CHAPTER TWENTY-FIVE | 175 |
| CHAPTER TWENTY-SIX | 187 |
| CHAPTER TWENTY-SEVEN | 192 |
| CHAPTER TWENTY-EIGHT | 199 |
| CHAPTER TWENTY-NINE | 203 |

# CHAPTER ONE

Julia was vexed beyond enduring. Stephen would not give her a divorce.

"Gossipmongers, windbags, jealous of our happiness, our love. Pay them no heed. That was not lip-rouge on my collar. The shawl you long ago misplaced is not now gracing the neck of the baker's wife. I must work late to maintain our lifestyle, to justify my elevation to president of the bank. Banish the thought of divorce from your mind. There is no cause for it. You are my wife, my treasured wife, now and forever."

Julia looked past the panes of the breakfast room window. Rustling skirts, bustling tradesmen, smiles, hearty handshakes. But there she was trapped behind glass, under glass really, for all to pity, distinguished not by talent but by fortitude, a martyred woman, the longsuffering philanderer's wife. She turned toward her treasured aunt, Lady Brighton.

"Stephen's in denial," sighed the older woman. "That was always his way when he was determined to justify some escapade. And my nephew now encourages you to do the same."

"I won't! I can't deny such a breach of our marriage vows."

"Believe me, it's best if you do. My dear Julia, no one will have you if you leave Stephen."

"I don't want anyone. Divorce will be my armor. I'll be left alone."

## SONDRA LUGER

"Alone is one thing. Alone in disrepute is another. You know I'm right, Julia. Make a life for yourself under the Lord Langley umbrella as you have, well, more of a life then. My nephew is not perfect, no man is. I had a taste of this myself, in earlier days. One must be realistic and practical. There is nothing to be gained by jumping off the metaphorical bridge."

"The reality and practicality of marriage should be based on mutual love, Aunt Margaret."

"That's not what the Church of England considers practical."

"I'm not the Church of England."

"Well, don't take it on, then. Take my advice, dear, and go along with the way things are, or you'll waste your life trying to change society."

Lady Brighton rose and kissed her niece goodbye. Julia watched her elderly aunt leave, then walked to the sofa, stretched out and dreamed of long ago.

Fifteen-year-old Julia Ann Geffen tumbled out of bed at the crowing of Matilda the rooster, slipped her feet into the cozy sheepskin slippers brother Jonathan had bought for her birthday, wrapped herself tightly in her wool robe and hurried through the chilly house. Her mother had just turned from lighting the wood in the living room's stone fireplace and stopped her with a "Good morning, darling," and a kiss on the cheek. The air was crisp and cool and behind the mountains, regal in the distance, a pale glow, a peak of morning sun to come. Her father was already in the field, with the springtime crops just beginning to peak their heads through the soil. Julia moved quickly to the barn, where Daisy the cow awaited her for milking. The chickens clucked a morning greeting, and Majestic, her horse, grunted. He hadn't had his breakfast. In a few hours Julia would ride him to Merivale, to make her monthly selection at the traveling library. She would bring home adventures set in other times, with other people and other places, after enjoying tea with Merivale friends. She would fill the rest of the day with indoor and outdoor tasks, and dreaming. It had all started then, that year, her father John's progress from tenant father to landowner to gentleman. Her mother no longer lit the fireplace. There were now servants for that. There was also less cooking and less cleaning from the mistress of the house. But Mama still clung to preparing special dishes for special occasions. Laboring in the kitchen was a joy to her. The rise in social status had its rewards, but also its social obligations and its loses. Julia's elementary, hard-working and joyous childhood was replaced with something more and something less. So it was when at age eighteen at the traveling library in Merivale she met a handsome man ten years her senior, whose grumbling about being stuck in this rural town was replaced by his pleasure in a sweet-faced, peach-complexioned girl who was intelligent, charming and forthright, devoid of guile and pretense. His lame horse became a blessing, and he returned the following year and the next to renew acquaintance with Julia Ann Geffen. Knowing only his pedigree and charm, at the urging of family and friends she married him. It was a fairy tale marriage at first - summers at his father's estate, winters in London, nature, culture, entertainment. What more could a young girl want? Julia sighed. She had rather hoped for love.

Stephen, Lord Langley, was the younger son of his father, treated handsomely when he tossed his parentage at would-be employers - what a coup to have him on staff - until his status as son number two was revealed, and his opportunities blighted. He found himself living on the proverbial shoestring, his man-about-town hopes dashed, though sporadically revived by financial additions to his coffer by his father, guilty for producing more than one son, and aware of the financial neglect it would legally entail. But when Julia Geffen came to London to the theater as an annual birthday treat accorded her by her parents, Stephen's prospects improved. The lovely Julia, all gussied up and smartly dressed, was the cynosure of all eyes wherever she went. And when Stephen was moved to escort her and her equally well-turned-out Mum to dining spots and places of pleasure, he attracted attention too. He urged the duo to come to London more often as his guest, Papa Langley's remittances being saved for these occasions. The gleams of envy and respect he had enjoyed at her appearances grew, as did his job titles. The bank clerk went from second assistant to first assistant, and upon his marriage to Julia Ann Geffen, with all who socially mattered in attendance, to bank president. Beautiful, charming, intelligent women mattered in London, the culture capital of England, and those in close proximity to them mattered too. And so it was that the fairy-tale courtship and marriage came to be and ended. The Beau Brummel spark in young Lord Langley emerged, and his good looks whetted the appetites of bored wives who envisioned themselves in Julia's place, enjoying the attentions they assumed he lavished on her. Discretion was paramount for Stephen and his lady-of-the-moment, so trumpeting of these affairs was avoided. Instead, rumor prevailed. Julia wasn't sure which was worse. But she remained the admired wife of Lord Langley and he remained a respected member of London society and the envy of London husbands for his acquisition of Julia and other women to his liking, even unbeknownst to them, some of their own wives.

"Yes," thought Julia, "I am property to be retained and flaunted." Lady Brighton thought this was the most she could expect. Even her mother's letters echoed this sentiment. Of course, if divorce was impossible, she could always leave Stephen, but could she extort money from her father for her eternal support? Could she behave as Stephen did and live on the largesse of another Romeo? She could open a boarding house, as unmarried or widowed matrons sometimes did, to support herself. What else was a woman alone to do? Her maid entered with a "Pardon me," to request instructions for the evening dinner. Julia looked out the window once more. She would attend to the matter of dinner and then hurry out for her weekly jaunt into the past. She would enjoy a mid-day repast at the Farmer's Market and be sustained once more by her dreams.

******

Julia changed to a simple white dress, donned a pale green bonnet to match her shoes and left the house.

Mayfair was posh, and as she walked the streets, she received no greetings from neighbors. This always amazed and slightly thrilled her, as she passed for just another maiden a working girl, carrying a covered basket to enclose provisions she had been sent to purchase. The street turned to cobblestones as she entered a tradesman's area where fresh fruits and vegetables were honestly displayed. It was one o'clock and the crowds had abated. She could mingle with ordinary people and move about with more freedom than at other hours. Today she wanted peaches, fuzzed and sweet for an entree preceded by an appetizer of grapes with a mini-loaf of old Mrs. Dawson's homemade bread. All would be washed down with Tommy's ale. Two more blocks and her basket would be filled with the elements of her feast.

The vendors smiled and chatted. They knew her, but not by name.

"The manure used make these the finest grapes in the county, lassie."

"Our peaches the finest always, as you know, dearie."

"Almost gone, but I saved a loaf for you."

Just one more stop. A pint of Tommy's ale and she would find a bench at the nearby square and enjoy her meal as she watched the world, the real world of hard-working men and women walk by. She would eat and sketch them, relaxing with a pastime that had given her pleasure since her youth. She had so enjoyed those times and the camaraderie with Dad when they sat and chatted at days end and she shared his ale. She missed him so, missed the life of nature and hard work, but she knew she wouldn't, couldn't exchange the life of comfort and culture she had now for that. Why couldn't she have it all, why must choices be made? But here, in one corner of her week she could replicate the simple pleasures of the past. Her timing was good. The bench she sought was empty at this hour. She took out her sketch pad and opened her basket. She took a sip of Tommy's ale, broke off a bit of Dora Dawson's moist and chewy bread and popped a grape into her mouth. A slight thump on the bench told her she had company. A young man in workmen's clothes was opening a leather pouch. He extracted a bunch of grapes and began tossing them one by one into the air and catching each in his mouth. His aim was good.

"We're of the same mind, I see," he said.

Julia did not respond. One did not speak to strangers unless properly introduced, and there was no one of accepted social order to make an introduction. And certainly a woman, a married woman, no less, was not about to introduce herself. She continued eating her grapes. A grape rolled at the toe of her right foot. "Sorry," came the voice of her bench-mate. Suddenly a face was looking up at hers, with deep, merry blue eyes. The young man retrieved the errant grape and tossed it six feet into the waste receptacle.

"Nice shoes," he said. "Just about the color of the apple I'm about to eat. I have an extra. Would you like it? It's just the thing to eat with Dora's bread and wash down with Tommy's ale. The peach would do nicely after."

He had been watching her! Julia froze in motion, a grape in hand. She turned upon him the glare that had halted greater men.

"I say, you can speak to me, you know. It's daylight. There's no danger. I'm new to London, a country boy. If my manners are deficient, please tell me. I'm eager to learn."

Julia closed her basket and rose, but now an errant grape of hers fell to the ground. The young man was quick to retrieve it.

"Must keep London clean."

Julia turned to go.

"I say, at least wish me good day. I can't have offended you too much for that."

She turned to the expectant face. She'd been a fool. She looked the lady's maid. Her face softened.

"Good day."

"Thank you. You have a lovely voice," he shouted as she hurried away.

The faces that she passed, that had warmed her on past market day excursions were now a blur. She had seen this young man the week before and he had followed her this very day. He had dared approach and speak to her. She looked at her hand and stopped in shock so suddenly that a man carrying a large jug nearly disengaged the basket from her hand. She had forgotten to put on her wedding ring. She had been fair game, a servant such as he, possibly in some lordship's home. Had she become so uppity that she disparaged as well as envied the social class of which not many years before she had been a part? She had made a choice with the wrong man, but a lifestyle choice she would not turn back even if she could. There were little ways to make the unpalatable sides work, market days for one, but Aunt Margaret was right. Why was Lady Brighton always right? She would indeed have to create the life she wanted as best she could under the Langley parasol, hopefully not an umbrella, if the philandering would abate. Stephen was good to her, which was more than most women could say of their husbands, and perhaps some with whom he dallied hoped to be in her place someday. But Stephen would not undergo the trouble, the expense, and worse yet the embarrassment of divorce, so her position was safe. Safety in marriage and being Lady Langley should be enough. The privileges, the adulation, the respect should be enough. She must stop thinking that it was not. The cobblestones were now far behind her as she completed the flagstone walk to the Langley home. She would wash down the day marred by the intrusive young man and the too wise Lady Brighton with a visit to her dear friend Georgina, Lady Willie, Lady Brighton's daughter.

## CHAPTER TWO

Visit days to Georgina were not planned. They just happened. Georgina liked it that way.

The unexpected was a salve to Lady Willie, who relished intrusions into days circumscribed by household duties, three children, and a sometimes-unruly staff, who adored her but often sidestepped her commands. Her peers adored her as well, and affectionately called the good-natured but often scatterbrained woman, out of her hearing, of course, Willy-Nilly. After the brazen approach of a servant and a scolding from Lady Brighton the counter that Georgina offered Julia was welcome. Julia scribbled a note, rang for Reggie, her footman, and requested prompt delivery to her friend. She changed her garments for more elegant attire and finished the repast interrupted on the bench, which prepared her for the ten-minute walk to the Willie mansion. It was almost on the outskirts of London, where more spacious dwellings could be acquired, and where larger families and their neighbors felt more comfortable with household clattering and noisy broods.

Julia's modest door knock was followed by one more vigorous, which resulted in the door being opened by the first-floor housemaid, her cap askew and two Willie boys clutching her apron and clamoring for her immediate return to the Great Hall. Julia followed the trio to the half size gig replica that lay wounded on the floor, the butler ordering the maid to rejoin him and hold the wagon wheel so he could weld the broken parts together. She obliged, and the boys watched fascinated as the repair was made, but downcast when they were told that tomorrow was the earliest they could ride it along the pathway to the house or the yard reserved for it in the rear.

"It's just as well, my darlings. The horse needs a rest and repair beyond what our James can effect. I'm off to the carpenter's shop to fetch him straightaway to replace Dobbie's front leg. Help Warfield and Hannah move the gig and Dobbie to the playroom. Yes, oh lovely, you're doing well."

Some slight chaos followed the group as they disappeared down the hall. Georgina turned to her friend.

"Well, Julia, are you ready for a trek? Oh, what am I thinking. You've just had one! James!" she called. He appeared. "Prepare the carriage, the full-size one, that is, for a ride to Smythe's shop." He began to speak, but she interrupted. "I know the footman can deliver the message, but then I'd have no reason for leaving the house, would I?"

Warfield smiled, bowed and went to summon the footman for the ride into town.

"You haven't been to town today, my friend, have you?"

Julia smiled and said nothing, which her friend took as agreement. Her weekly incognito market walk was a private matter meeting a private need which she preferred to share with no one, not even dear Georgina. Too many questions would arise to accompany the revelation.

Georgina peered through the window. "The gig's in place and we're off!" Warfield opened the front door and helped the women into the vehicle, and they were off indeed.

"Oh my dear friend, I couldn't do this with anyone else. Mother is aghast at how I treat your visits. But I adore her, as I know you do." She patted Julia's hands. "And she is a wonderful grandmama, always bringing sweets and other treats to the children when she comes each week, in late afternoon, of course, after nuncheon, and after the children have exhausted themselves in play. But she had her share of child-raising and deserves a more restful time with her grandchildren, though I was not the handful that I have produced."

Smythe's response to Lady Willie's frequent requests were always as prompt as they were lucrative. She instructed the footman to return with the gig in two hours.

"Plenty of time to do whatever we want to do. What shall today's adventure be?"

"The library, perhaps?"

"Splendid! A London Lady's latest romance arrives today, and the librarian has me atop the list of borrowers. Cook requested THE FRENCH COOK when next I go, so I'll get that too. Then we'll have a spot of tea as we await the carriage."

"You know the Gilbert sisters will be there with the latest gossip."

"Is Monday their library day?" Georgina asked innocently, but with a twinkle in her eyes.

******

They were helped from the carriage, and walked to the entrance of the most elegant and expensive subscription library in London. Inside the silence was refreshing. The noise that was the hallmark of London streets was gone, replaced by murmurs. Georgina headed immediately to the cookbook section to make sure that other dazzling titles did not cause her to forget Cook's request for Louis Ude's book, then on to the history section to peruse what was new, what distant worlds were available to enter for relaxation and excitement. She left the best for last, the romance section, before joining others chatting sotto voce with the Gilbert sisters at the beginning of the checkout line. The librarian's raised hand to Georgina indicated that the romance she sought awaited her.

Julia's survey of the library's offerings began with the natural science bookcase, at which she lingered, before she continued on to briefly survey other sections before setting her reticule down on a table near the music section. She was engrossed in perusing a book from a shelf when a voice behind her spoke.

"You mustn't take that book. You'll never learn to play the mandolin from that. I know, I tried."

Julia turned to face the man from the bench. "Perhaps I'm a better reader of instructions than you are."

"Indeed." He bowed to her retort. "Women of breeding play the piano. Hasn't your mistress told you that?"

Julia held the book fast and turned away. She retrieved her reticule and headed quickly to the fiction section across the room. The young man followed.

"Ah, fictional romance, no doubt. The piano will really do better for success in this area. Until you marry, of course. Then no one will care what you play, though whist, I hear, is currently popular with the female married set."

Julia turned to face him, her fury barely contained. "I shall call the librarian if you continue to follow me. It's a wonder you gained entry to this library. I doubt if you're a member of this or any reputable book establishment."

The young man pulled a card from his pocket. "I have a pass." He waved it before her face.

Julia turned abruptly, the point of her parasol digging deeply into the man's foot, as she hurried to Georgina's side at the checkout counter. The young man emitted a howl of pain, which was not appreciated by the browsers, whose facial expressions, upon their survey of his person, made it clear that he was hardly one of them.

"Was that dreadful young man bothering you, Julia?"

"He was advising me on what to read."

"What is the world coming to? Servants do not advise their betters. But it would be like kindly Lord Tilton to employ a man like that. He feels for the underprivileged and unemployed, and the rest of us sometimes suffer for his choices. This young man is a temporary replacement for his handyman, who was called away on a family health issue. Robert told me he arrived two weeks ago and will stay at least through Christmas, no longer if London is lucky. You would think he would at least dress appropriately when entering this establishment."

"Let's hope for all our sakes that his stay here is a short one, and while he is here he should often be out of sight. He surely has work to do. I saw you talking to the Gilbey sisters. Any news we should be aware of?"

"Yes, Julia," laughed Georgina. "Wishing to hear news sounds like a respectable request. I'll tell you over tea." And clutching their respective volumes the ladies left the domain of "Silent Please" for a teatime chat and the latest gossip.

# CHAPTER THREE

Lady Willie observed that one teapot might not be sufficient for the Gilbey news.

"It seems that the export-import business is rife with more than tea, porcelain and exotic fabrics. More than one husband is flirting with the female purveyors of goods and more than one wife the males! My Robert seems to be one of the few decent members of the lot, and the Gilbeys agree. I will no longer examine the wares at Chancy's Porcelain Shop until he stops examining the wares of other men's wives! If enough of us do the same he'll change his ways. The purse speaks louder than verbal reprimands."

Julia nodded agreement. "A London Lady does well to advise wives of the activities of their reprobate husbands."

"Yes, indeed, but it's easier to point out failure than to rectify it, though she does make suggestions. We may have to change our milk carrier as well."

"Did she hint that Stephen —"

"No, Julia, and you must drop this fixation that idle rumors are accurate."

"You mean only intimations in the stories of A London Lady are to be trusted?"

"Well, you know her accuracy is uncanny. The noticeable changes in the London elite after they've been slyly mentioned in one of her stories proves it."

"Will she ever run out of dirt to reveal?"

"What do you think! At least you and I are safe. We've avoided her knife these seven years. She seems to have finished despoiling us. Only the newbies on the scene now appear to be in danger of her thrust."

"A London Lady does a service, but at a price. A marriage can never be the same once an infidelity is revealed. A woman's heart remembers. Even if forgiveness is dispensed, the heart remembers. A London lady is the conscience of London. She must make a fortune from her work."

"Gyles Ford would love to know who her printer is. My Robert tells me that he believes London exposés should properly be printed in London, preferably by him. He has traced the paper and the bindery to a French printer, whose mouth is sealed."

"She can't be French herself; she knows too much about London. Many Parisians do come here during the Season, but she would have to live here to know what she knows and have spies in all the businesses and private homes. She must be wealthy to afford the expense."

"We may never know her identity, only the activities of those whose misbehavior she brings to light. I'll let you know the details after I read the book. Don't frown, Julia. You must stop thinking Stephen has betrayed you. He's good to you, and he performs his functions well, does he not?"

"Less performance and more sincerity would be welcome. The scents so often on his collar are not mine."

"Whose are they, do you think?"

"They vary, so they must belong to Legion."

"Well there, you see. You're the only constant in Stephen's life. Have you spoken to Mother?"

"Yes, your mother, Stephen and God Almighty. Only God Almighty understands."

"Don't even think the 'D' word, my friend. If it were possible and financially do-able, so many wives would run for the exits the country would be undone. Have children, Julia. They're such a solace."

"Not with Stephen."

"Good heavens, not with someone else!"

Julia laughed. "No, dear Georgina, though I'm sure you are right. A child, a son especially, might distract him from his escapades, and a daughter might lead him to consider that he would not want a poacher to despoil her."

"You shouldn't wait much longer. Think of it, a little one with your qualities."

"Or Stephen's. Well, he does have some good ones."

"There, then, that's settled. I'm delighted with my brood of three, and so is Robert."

"Settled," thought Julia, shaking her head.

******

Georgina looked at her watch. "The carriage should arrive soon. Just time to buy flowers for the bedroom vase. We have tons of flowers in the garden, but they're for the common areas of the house. These will be personal, just for Robert and me."

Julia sighed. She was happy that her friend was happy.

They crossed the street to the flower vendor on the corner. Georgina bought some roses and Julia some camellias. "Just for myself," Julia thought.

"Perfect timing," exclaimed Georgina, as her carriage arrived. They crossed to the cafe, the footman helped them in, and the trot home began.

"Robert and I have your dinner party to look forward to. Who are the new London couple you've invited?"

"Thomas and Matilda Evans. Stephen admires their bank account, I mean their reputation. They've put a small amount in Stephen's bank, and are considering moving more from their holdings in America. Lord Tilton and Amy will also be there."

Georgina laughed. "You do well to link their names together, at least from Lord Tilton's viewpoint, but I doubt he will be able to convince the wealthy widow to marry him. She wants someone looser with the purse-strings, so she needn't untie hers. I rather think she likes her independence, and is enjoying the attentions of her many suitors. Lord Tilton will have to be less verbal and more tangibly lavish to even have a prayer of winning her. "

"Stephen has an eye to winning more of his account as well. He keeps it at his country seat. He says he is wary of London banks. Amy has a tidy sum Stephen would like to control as well."

"I thought this was to be a purely social event?"

"A social event it surely is, but nothing is pure these days."

The horses clomped to a halt at Julia's house and she was assisted in her descent from the carriage.

"Until tomorrow, then, Georgina." And her friend waved as the horses galloped off.

Julia mused that her husband would be home soon and she would do well to change into an evening ensemble for dinner. He was a punctual man and did not like to be kept waiting. She had just donned a pale blue shift and white wrap when the downstairs maid approached her, hurried and harried. A note had arrived informing the girl that her mother had taken ill and required a bit of help and cheering. The dining room required dusting. It was clean, but Lord Tilton's allergies — the silverware needed polishing and the curtains needed to be changed before tomorrow's dinner. Maggie had been expected to attend to them, but she had only one hour to catch the coach. Julia could not deny her request. No need to tell Stephen. He considered housework more important than a housemaid's family. In the morning Julia would polish, clean and dust. Hadn't she done these things in years long past? They would remind her of her progress in life. She needed to be reminded that it was progress. Cook would not appreciate a request that she do more than she had signed on for. Tonight she and Stephen would eat Mrs. North's excellent dinner, and Julia would listen to her husband's avid, eager, energetic accounts of his day. Her excursions to Georgina, the library, the cafe would not be heard, so her pleasures were safe in her heart. Stephen would never ask.

# CHAPTER FOUR

The day dawned bright and clear, just right for the tasks Julia had set for herself before the evening do. London in autumn was a wonderful place to be. For a man, parliament, politics and economic activity. For a woman, theatre, fashion and friends, current, new, and rediscovered, for all the world descended on the city, to enjoy its victuals, its entertainments, and its vices. The house accounts were in order, the window pane repaired and the roof leak attended to. An interesting assortment of guests would grace the Langley table this evening. All was well in the Langley world.

First to arrive that evening were Mr. and Mrs. Thomas Evans, fresh from America but a fortnight ago. They made a quiet entrance, the missus carefully scanning her surroundings and hosts. Next to arrive were Lord Tilton and Amy Burton, Tilton smiling serenely and Amy with bright and happy greetings. And last, Georgina and Robert, he calm and pleasant and she bubbling with enthusiasm and joy and spreading the salutary effect to the previous arrivals. Half an hour of pleasantries in the drawing room was followed by all repairing to the dining room. The Evanses were astonished by the display of food before them, not the way in America.

"How is it in the colonies, these days?" asked Lord Tilton.

"I wouldn't know," replied Evans. "I lived in the United States of America, which was doing well when we left."

"Sorry," said Lord Tilton.

"That they are no longer colonies, or that you forgot," laughed Georgina.

The laughter that joined hers was awkward and light.

Soup, which began the meal, was followed by a small salad and cheese, which was succeeded by a large joint of beef, surrounded by various platters of game, pickles, jelly and vegetables, and followed in conclusion by an assortment of custards and puddings. Mrs. Evans, forewarned of the abundance, though not of its extent, ate lightly, saving space for the peach melba and syllabub. Georgina's animation in discussing the latest Paris fashions nearly caused an instant new design on Mrs. Evans' formal frock, but Robert caught the syllabub before it landed on her lap. He wiped his hand nonchalantly on his napkin without a break in his conversation on the new income tax they were now saddled with.

"I'm thinking of closing up the windows in the servants' quarters, Stephen," joked Lord Tilton. "The window tax is outrageous."

"We put in one window less when we built our house five years ago," noted Robert.

"I rent," observed Thomas Evans.

"You're lucky you don't have children, Mr. Evans. You'd need a spacious residence, windows and all," replied Stephen.

"Lucky is not a word I'd use," said Robert.

"Oh, yes," laughed Stephen, "You have three."

"Any thoughts of increasing your number from zero?" asked Robert.

"That's a question for Julia," Stephen replied uneasily.

"We have a magnificent English setter," offered Mr. Evans.

## SONDRA LUGER

Robert bit his tongue to keep from laughing. "Not quite the same," he responded. The meal concluded, the gentlemen remained in the dining room for a smoke and more talk of politics and the rising cost of living, which segued into the advantages of investing wisely and banking with Lord Langley. The women repaired to the drawing room to chat of this and that. "This" consisting of keeping house in London, and "that" consisting of London life during the season. They were in the midst of discussing the theatre and musical events in the West End.

"Passive entertainment is enjoyable," said Mrs. Evans, but in the 'colonies,' "she laughed," participation is equally appreciated. Is dancing in order during the Season, if not outside the home at least within it? After feasts such as you served this evening, Lady Langley, dancing would be welcome."

"We have many venues for dancing, Mrs. Evans, but here at home, well — we have no piano. If we bought one we would need guests who could play, because I can't. Of course, I could learn, but —"

"Oh, I forgot," inserted Amy, "I was to suggest to you the mandolin. Lord Tilton has a new servant for the season who plays the mandolin, very well, I must say. He thinks you'd find the mandolin a pleasant addition to your dinner parties."

Mrs. Evans looked gratified at Mrs. Burton's support.

"He likes the young man," continued Amy, "and would like to see him supplement his wages. Heaven forbid he himself should pay him more. He thought the suggestion would be more appealing coming from me than from him."

The clock sounded the hour and delayed Julia's response enough for her to avoid making one. The men entered the drawing room to retrieve their women.

"A hearty good night. It was a pleasure having you all," announced Julia.

The butler opened the door and the guests, offering profuse appreciation for the evening, departed, their coaches awaiting them on the street.

"I'm always amazed that some believe business and pleasure have to be separated." said Stephen, rubbing his hands together. "This evening brought me a new client. The Evanses are charming people are they not?"

"That's a bit of a stretch," laughed Julia.

"Just charming," continued Stephen. "Oh, and by the way, have you thought of learning to play the mandolin?"

# CHAPTER FIVE

Edward Riley bent low and stood awkwardly before Julia in the Langley library. He was the persistent young man from the market and the library.

"Please forgive me, Lady Langley. I was not aware of your identity. It will be a privilege to share my knowledge of the mandolin with you."

Julia said nothing and turned her back to him for a moment. She was determined to be difficult.

"Surely at the farmer's market, at least, you can understand my error. You dressed as — others do."

Julia turned to face him. "Then you judge women by their dress? Does demeanor, reserve and obvious disposition mean nothing to you?"

"I am merely a man, your ladyship, and men often lack the wisdom of the fairer sex."

"Well said," thought Julia. Now relaxed, she laughed.

"What brought you to an interest in the mandolin?"

"Music is a balm to nourish the soul, and the mandolin is a mellow and sweet instrument, useful as well for musical soirées at home. I am past the piano, being no longer a maiden, and I thought it less expensive, more portable and less difficult to master."

"That it is. However, I don't believe age or marital status should inform one's decision as to what musical instrument to play, but I would certainly despair of your enduring a dislocated back after you transported a piano to another venue."

Julia smiled. "I appreciate your concern for my health. Now, shall we begin?"

Edward Riley's chair faced Julia's as he demonstrated how to hold the instrument. He rose and inserted a thin parchment beneath the strings of her mandolin incasing the names of the strings. As he plucked and played each one over and over, the repetition nearly felled Julia's lady's maid, assigned as chaperone for the event. Sitting in a corner she began to close her eyes and she nearly fell from her seat. Mr. Riley explained, demonstrated and had Julia follow suit. He moved his chair next to hers to more easily correct her errors. The hour flew by, and the light snoring of the chaperone alerted them to the time.

"Would this time next week be satisfactory for us to continue our lessons?"

"Yes. How long do you think it will be before i can play a complete piece properly?"

"That's hard to say, but you have grasped the essentials well, so relatively soon, I would guess."

"Would you like to hear what I'm sure you will have mastered before I leave Lord Tilton's employ at month's end?'

She was eager to hear.

The young man looked at his mandolin silently for a moment, lifted his face to Julia's and began to play. Julia was transfixed by the beauty of his playing, and as the last notes hung in the air sat motionless before breaking into applause, which aroused the maid.

"You have an ear for quality and the ability to reproduce it. Where did you learn the pleasures of the mandolin?"

"I work on Lord Kendall's estate, and I was exposed to it there. I am delighted my playing has pleased you. In a short while I expect your playing to please me and your guests, should you choose to honor them with your gifts."

"I hardly think I have displayed any gifts."

"No, but you have gifts which will result in its reflection when you play the mandolin."

"May I ask what you think my gifts are?"

"Liveliness and tenderness."

"Opposites."

"Yes, and yet not so. You can go in both directions at once."

Julia laughed. "I am truly unique."

"I hope your husband appreciates that," said Edward, and he quickly bowed and made his exit, the maid following.

His departure was followed soon after by the arrival of her husband. His perfunctory kiss on the cheek was concluded with a walk to the library.

"Have Mrs. North bring my dinner to the library. I've so much work yet to do. "Sorry, darling, you'll have to eat alone."

But if Julia was to eat alone, she preferred to do it in her bedchamber, where private thoughts were more appropriate. The music lesson had been a lesson indeed. A man had shared music with her, taught her, listened to her, appreciated her. It had been a long time since she had enjoyed such attention from a man. She massaged her mandolin warmly. The proprietor of the music shop on Mount Street had shown her the range of mandolins he had available. He had relayed to her the recommendations relayed to him by her instructor, who had been there the day before, suggestions that would assist her in determining the instrument she would feel must comfortable to play, look at and enjoy. She had selected the instrument sitting on her lap, which would spend the night with her and give her sweet dreams. Rumors were a plentiful commodity in London. No post was necessary to transport them. They were spread by the servants even the middle class were able to employ and provided entertainment at no charge throughout the city. A handsome young man instructing Lady Langley on the mandolin would never make it to the press, which was loathe to upset the elite. The gossipmongers would do that if there was cause, and these days cause was determined by a woman, identity unknown, who incorporated fact in the fiction she wrote as A London Lady. This mysterious paragon of moral virtue had not alighted on the actual transgressions of Stephen, Lord Langley, and was hardly likely to seize upon idle gossip about a teacher and his student. She had a seven-year record of accuracy founded upon substance, not fairy tales. But Julia was not in the mood for reality. She opened the latest novel of her favorite author, anonymous, too, but of a different stripe. She knew that in the pages of EMMA truths would be revealed and wrongs would be righted. In the real world she could only hope for the same. The world of fiction was a much safer world to inhabit. She read for an hour before extinguishing the candle, snuggling beneath the comforter and dropping off to sleep.

******

In the morning, after assessing household needs and informing the staff of new tasks she wished done, Julia prepared for her weekly visit to the Maltby mansion. The caretaker was an old woman who appreciated her visits and whose company she enjoyed. The Maltby mansion was just outside London, too great a walk for the old woman who had no coach to whisk her to the pleasures and liveliness of London. No one came to visit. She had no friends that Julia knew of and led a solitary existence there. Why the heirs, who apparently were distant nephews, had not sold the Maltby estate, was a puzzle which could not be solved, because there were no servants living there to spread news, real or concocted, which would explain why the grounds continued to be maintained by itinerant workers and the mansion by a lone elderly woman for half the year. Perhaps they couldn't agree on what to do. But seven years was a long time to endure the expense of maintaining a mansion none of them seemed to want to inhabit. Of course, an elderly woman hired to dust and clean the mansion for six months of the year would not be a great expense. Julia had visited Elsie a fortnight earlier, and felt remiss in not returning sooner. A fortnight without companionship would be displeasing to Julia, but Elsie seemed not to mind, perhaps because a messenger from London regularly delivered her groceries and whatever other provisions she required, but he was only a brief presence once a week. Julia's offer, which had angered Stephen, to bring her into town weekly in the Langley barouche had been roundly refused. Elsie would not, she said, inconvenience anyone, even for a short while, especially the young woman who had befriended her, and what would her husband think? Elsie was apparently psychic. It was a cool and clear autumn day, and Julia reflected that the countryside would be ablaze with red, orange and yellow leaves. She looked forward to the ride and the scenery. She would request Reggie to remain to drive her home. Surely once a week, she had told Stephen, to the outskirts of London would not tire the horses or cause them distress requiring a veterinarian's attention. The barouche had been purchased mainly for business trips by the banker and for impressing prospective clients, but it was also used for transporting the couple to evening social events in the city, and murmurs of discontent from Lord Langley were then few, and totally absent when the social event held the prospect of obtaining a new client.

Elsie had seen Julia's arrival from a window, and hurried out to greet her friend.

"What a delight to see you, my dear. Two baskets for nuncheon! Oh, you shouldn't have, you needn't have. I have provisions enough for us both."

"Not like these. You've never tasted such peaches, and the wine and cheeses are imported and rare."

"You are a darling." She squeezed Julia's hand. "You're determined to spoil me."

"You deserve spoiling. You spend so much time in and around the house I thought a barouche ride on this beautiful day would be refreshing, and munching and chatting under a majestic oak or elm would be just the thing."

"Splendid!" The old woman took a light wrap from the hall closet, tied a bonnet under her chin, and holding Julia's hand descended the mansion steps to the waiting vehicle.

They sat in silence, smiling at the passing landscape, inhaling the scented breeze until Reggie alerted them to a commanding oak hiding behind overgrown shrubbery a short distance off the side of the road. He carried the two baskets to the spot, spread the blankets, laid out the provisions and eased Elsie into position to enjoy the repast. Elsie gasped at the fine China, utensils and napkins, far above the quality she used daily.

"You are so thoughtful! Bless you, my dear."

The chats of the old woman and the young matron always began with the latest news gleaned by Elsie from her subscription to the London Press.

"Expensive, but worth it. What else do I have to spend my money on?"

Talk then segued into London news beyond what the newspaper relayed, courtesy of Julia. It was about people of whom the old woman could have no knowledge, but which she heard with interest. Their conversations always ended with reminiscences of earlier days, happy, youthful days. Both had been born on farms and relished the pleasures of the land and the work. Neither spoke of their personal lives, of their marriages, any unpleasantness that had befallen them. Their time spent together was idyllic. Julia realized how much she needed her friends, her loving, realistic, but no-nonsense aunt Lady Brighton, the sensible, endearingly awkward Lady Willie and the lovely, caring Elsie. The ride back to the Maltby mansion was filled with song, favorites of the past, until a bull romping through some sycamore trees prompted Julia to begin a story of her youth. As they mounted the steps of the Maltby mansion a gig approached and stopped behind Julia's barouche. A banana peeking through one of the baskets the young man carried revealed that Elsie's weekly grocery delivery had arrived. The delivery boy repaired to the kitchen with them and returned to the gig to retrieve a packet of envelopes. Julia was surprised, but gratified.

"At least your family hasn't forgotten you."

Elsie laughed and put the packet face down on the table.

"You must finish your story about the bull that invaded your garden and frightened your six year-old self. But first I must put away these perishables. I'll meet you in the morning room."

As Elsie hastened to the kitchen, Julia began to walk to the morning room. But she halted and returned to the foyer. Curiosity had gotten the better of her. She turned the packet face up. The only writing on the top envelope was one word and initials - "From JB." She turned up the second envelope. it was from "Jerom." This was an odd way of addressing envelopes. There was no postage on them and no possibility that they came from distant clan, and the packet was at least two inches thick.

She looked up at the elegant portrait of the late Lady Maltby. "What do you think of this?" She received no response. Julia turned the envelopes face down again and repaired to the morning room. She realized that delivery boys do not deliver mail.

Elsie smiled as she returned with a plate of cookies and a pot of tea. Julia finished the story about the bull, and after some parting pleasantries and a hug and a kiss took leave of her friend. As the barouche carried her home, Julia rebuked her curiosity about Elsie's mail.

"We all have secrets," she silently declared, as the horses clattered down the road, past dear Georgina's house and entered London proper. "I've never spoken of Stephen more than superficially, nor she of her husband. We've been friends for five years. and that's all I need to know. More is none of my business."

## CHAPTER SIX

The next day brought a delightful surprise. Julia had just finished an hour of practice on the mandolin and had just settled in to reading in the library when Jameson entered with a message that had just arrived from the Tilton mansion. Julia lifted it from the tray, broke the seal and read the invitation to attend a concert that very night that included a performance by a respected mandolin musician. Edward Riley had come into possession of two orchestra tickets and was offering them to Julia and Stephen. When Stephen returned home Julia could barely contain her excitement as she relayed the news. In three hours they could be enjoying a musical end to the evening.

"I'm sorry Julia, but I've much to do tonight. I can't spare the time to attend. Perhaps Lord Tilton could escort you, as it was he who suggested you learn to play the mandolin."

"Oh, Stephen, can't the work wait?"

"Such pleasure must not be mine tonight. I have responsibilities to shoulder to our investors and our customers, and they must take precedence over the mandolin. After dinner I must work through the night."

Dinner was spoiled for Julia, as she numbly heard Stephen recount the details of his day. After dinner Stephen went to the library to work, with a request that he not be disturbed. Julia was about to ascend the stairs to her bedchamber when Jameson delivered another note. it was a response to her reply to Edward Riley, but it was from Lord Tilton. He offered to escort her to the concert and would not accept a refusal. He would come by to do so at 7:30.

Julia quickly penned her reply. "Thank you, my darling friend. I await your arrival," and she hurried to her bedchamber to dress for the occasion.

******

The Hanover Square Rooms were buzzing with anticipation of the performances by the reputed ensemble and their guest soloist, playing the mandolin. Lady Langley and Lord Tilton were given their programs and escorted to their seats.

"Thank you for getting me out of the house, Gerald. Stephen's work claims his attention day and night."

"The thanks are due Edward Riley. I am merely his fortunate replacement."

"These seats are costly. I hope Edward was not unduly put out by the expense."

"It gave him pleasure to make the sacrifice."

Beethoven, Mozart and Handel were on the program, with Mozart and Beethoven doing honors for the mandolin. The curtain rose and the audience quieted. The musicians entered the stage and opera glasses were raised to view them more closely. At intermission Lord Tilton led Julia to the Queens's Tea Room, and they sipped champagne and munched chips at a corner table that afforded them a good view of the intermission crowd. Lord Tilton was smiling at one of Julia's pleasantries when the smile froze. Julia turned to look in the direction of his gaze. Engrossed in conversation with a man she recognized as the owner of a jewelry concern was Amy Burton. The effect of this sight on Lord Tilton was extraordinary. He lost his ability to speak, able only to stutter incoherent replies to Julia's comments designed to divert his attention from the sight, and he turned paler than the white draperies in the room. He finally regained his voice.

"What has he to offer her?" he demanded. "A merchant dealing in overpriced goods, pretending them worthy of purchase by the elite. No breeding, no manners, no title. What can she see in him?"

"Gerald, it's only an evening out they're having."

"To honor him with her company, I never would have expected this of her."

"Dear Gerald, you know she sees other men."

"Well, she shouldn't!"

The finality of that statement left Julia with nothing to say.

"Stand up and wave!" he ordered.

Amy and her man had seen them and were waving to them as they skirted tables and groups of people to join them.

"I had no idea you were a fan of Beethoven and Mozart, Gerald."

Lord Tilton relaxed a bit. She didn't know, a reasonable explanation.

"He probably came for the Handel," her escort said.

Tilton's body stiffened, and Julia squeezed his hand to restrain him from replying.

The man eyed the Tilton tie. "Must keep up to date in fashion as well as music, m'lord."

The Tilton tie was old-school.

Tilton managed to ignore this. "I didn't know you were interested in tonight's concert, Amy. Why didn't you tell me?"

"It was Martin's idea. Julia, are you enjoying the concert?"

"Very much, and I look forward to hearing the mandolin selection. It should encourage me to apply myself to my instrument. You've heard I've begun mandolin lessons?"

"Yes, congratulations I'm sure — "

"We really must be getting back," interrupted Lord Tilton, as he took Julia by the elbow and pulled her away. He nodded his goodbye. He didn't trust himself to speak.

Julia was not sure Lord Tilton heard the rest of the program. His eyes were glazed, and only when the applause had ended and he accompanied her to the exit did any semblance of his usual regal demeanor return. His carriage was double-parked, along with many others, and as he heaved back in his seat he turned to Julia imploring eyes.

"Am I too old and foolish to win anyone so lively and sweet?"

"You are neither old nor foolish. Do not despair."

"In my youth maidens flocked to me from miles around. Have I lost the knack, or have things changed so much that I am out of touch with how to please a woman? These ten years without my bride have been hard. Am I destined to continue in loneliness? Is there no hope for me with Amy?"

"She must like you, dear friend, or she would not continue seeing you. Take heart in that."

"'Like' may be all I can hope for!"

"Do not think this way. Keep on keeping on. She must see you for the fine man you are. There is comfort in that."

## SONDRA LUGER

Horses and coaches flashed by in the darkness, lit intermittently by the street lamps, as they rode from London's West End to the upscale residential neighborhood that in the night looked as dark as all the rest. The coach stopped before Julia's house on Grosvenor Square, and Gerald walked her up the steps before a fond "Thank you, my dear, for this evening. Perhaps I will find a woman to light my life as Stephen has his."

"I thank you, dear Gerald." She kissed him lightly on the cheek. "My fervent prayers are for your success."

Julia closed the door and stood in the dark stillness until she heard the clomp of horses carry her escort away. Maggie had left a candle for her on the foyer table. She carried it to the library and peeked inside. Stephen had apparently finished his work, but he had missed a lovely concert. She moved to the staircase and had almost reached the top when she heard the door open. Stephen entered. He removed his jacket and his gloves. She hurried to her bedchamber, and with her back against the closed door, heard him ascend the stairs. His work had taken place beyond the library. She wondered who she was this week. It was mere curiosity; it really didn't matter. It was not his wife. She reflected that Gerald was having difficulty winning the woman of his dreams, and she was having difficulty getting rid of hers. She undressed in the candlelight. There would be no indication to Stephen that she was awake and aware. In the morning she would reflect once again on how to deal with her unfaithful husband.

# CHAPTER SEVEN

When Lady Brighton arrived for their weekly tea the next day, Julia unburdened her heart of the night before. She prefaced the information with the earlier pleasure of the evening and the confrontation that occurred when Amy Burton and her escort offered greetings at Intermission.

"Poor Gerald. A fine man, if a bit old-fashioned."

"Poor Julia as well," said Lady Langley. "I arrived home to discover that Stephen was not working in the library, as he had promised. When he arrived home I hastened to bed. You can imagine with whom and on whom he was working."

"I can only imagine the female of last night, but I can name the one of the week before. This morning, when I went to Dorrie's Bake shop for some of his delicious scones, he took me aside and begged for my help. He had forced his wife to confess, under threat of a household income reduction, that she had reneged on their marriage vows, and with some frequency, engaging in liaisons with Stephen. It has now become my civic duty or at least a necessity if I wish to frequent Dorrie's without shame, to put a stop to these occurrences. His wife will surely attempt to stop now, but she said Lord Langley was a persistent wretch, who might withdraw daily pastry deliveries to the bank staff. Dorrie's has regularly boasted of the honor of the bank patronage, and this has attracted a larger clientele. His is not the only good pastry shop in London, but I think it is the best."

"Did she call Stephen a wretch?"

"No, that was my amendment. We must devise a plan to stop his immoral outings. Women who lack a claim to royalty are flattered by his attention, his charm and his good looks, which overpower their loyalty to dull, unpretentious husbands. Yes, Julia, by observation and experience I have determined that most husbands leave a lot to be desired in the fascination department."

"How is this to be done?"

"If A London Lady were in pursuit of the story our task would be so much easier. If we close off entrance to the commodity, if Stephen's charm and title meet more resistance, we would have more time to devise a plan to curb the activities of the culprit himself. But we must first know how many and who these women are. My servants fraternize with those of other households and can be the gateway to the information we seek. A bonus may entice them. I shall tread carefully, of course. Lady Brighton, despite this spying engagement, must remain a lady still."

"Is Stephen worth all this bother?"

"No, dear, my nephew is not, but you are. You must be made as comfortable as possible for the next fifty or sixty years."

"Must is a frightening word, Aunt Margaret, need it be a 'must?'"

"It can be no other way. You either endure Stephen, and there are compensations, you must admit, or return to your parents or open a boarding house — a huge comedown and disgrace— or flee London to heaven-knows-where, with no means of support except what your parents may provide. Actually, Stephen, at first, was subsidized by his father until his rise to London prominence at the bank. But you, dear, have no route to prominence or survival without your parents or your husband. A woman is a second-class citizen without a first-class husband."

"If divorce were possible —"

"Don't talk nonsense, you know it's not. There have been only a handful of divorces in the past fifty years in all of England. Do you think Stephen could ever be persuaded to make the required appeal to Parliament, to get the Church of England to accept it, to endure the shame and absorb the enormous cost? I wish for your happiness, dearest, but you would not be happy as a divorced woman."

"If I remarried —"

"Darling, you are young and beautiful, but men do not rush to acquire used merchandise and beauty, alas, fades with time."

"But character —"

"Is vastly overrated as an appeal to men. We can both think of many mismatched marriages in that regard. We shall find a way to make you happy, not as happy as you would like, but sufficiently so to make living with Stephen worthwhile. Stephen's paramours shall be discovered and discouraged from choosing Stephen."

"Their identities may change."

"But the ones he particularly patronizes now, when they are discovered and — threatened is such a nasty word — will be a warning to those yet to come. Word of those apprehended will travel fast, and cuckolded husbands are not likely to take kindly to their betrayal."

"You assume these women are married."

"An assumption based on experience, Julia, the experience of hearing and seeing revealed decades of such liaisons. Stephen is not likely to venture to prostitutes. They would be damage to his ego. Winning what is prized by others is part of what makes this pastime worthwhile. Be patient. I will get the names of the women with whom he is involved and together we shall decide how to deal with them."

"So I must devote my time to punishment and meting out justice to assuage my betrayal?"

"Not all your time, dear. But you will be helping men who are betrayed. You will be righting the wrongs inflicted on them. You will be doing a public service."

"Like A London Lady," mused Julia. Her novellas have certainly had a salutary effect."

"They have indeed. Do not despair. We shall right things."

"You seem sure of success."

"One can't be sure of anything, but if we put our courage to the sticking place we shall not fail."

Julia laughed. "Shakespeare's Lady Macbeth. But she was contemplating murder."

"We won't be going that far, dear, but the effects on the culprits will be as if we had. I must be going now, but be of good cheer, for it is your father's good pleasure to give you the kingdom."

"A good biblical sentiment. Thank you, Aunt Margaret."

Lady Brighton waved the thanks away and departed.

"This is the best I can hope for," thought Julia, "but I am still perversely hoping for more. Still, there are happy times in the offing, my mandolin lessons with Edward, a new frock to be made from Robert, Lord Willie's, new supply of silks and satins, Christmas with my parents. And there are visits to be made to the indigent and ill. There is still good to be done in this world, and while I'm still in it I should have a hand in doing them."

The day was still young and the house was in order. Julia grabbed a bonnet and put on a blue jacket. She needed air. She needed more noise, more voices, lots of activity to drown out her troubled thoughts. Mount Street was the ticket, the streets leading to and from especially. A pinwheel spinning in the breeze atop a cart of toys attracted her attention, a bright orange scarf waved to her from the corner of a basket containing its cousins. Street cries alerted her to pastry, pamphlets, books on makeshift tables and stacked boxes. Street musicians begged for her attention and her coins. The street activity could distract you if you allowed it to, if you refused to see the poverty behind it, the sellers loudly and happily calling out their wares, sellers who could not afford to ply their trade in store fronts. You could buy everything on the street. You could brush against half of London on one trek. But Julia soon felt faint. The street cries had become unbearable noise. The air, never fresh in London, had become foul. She walked in search of empty streets and fresher air, walked and walked until she found herself not far from Georgina's home. The sky had turned dark and it depressed her. The straight path was the right one, the one that led to dear Georgina's door.

Georgina, Lady Willie, hair upswept in combs, straggling ends sweeping across her lovely face, opened the door.

"Julia, you look awful!"

"Thank you," came the faint reply. And the speaker collapsed.

"Warfield! Warfield!" shouted Lady Willie.

Her butler instantly responded to the call, his hands a tangle of rope from the young Master's hoop, which he was in the process of repairing. He carried the fainted woman to the morning room sofa and hastily repaired to the kitchen for water and spirits.

Julia sat up, grateful for the pillows Georgina was stuffing behind her back.

"I know it's not visiting day," she began, "I should have called."

"Visiting day be hanged! What happened to you?"

"Your mother came for conversation this morning."

"One-way, no doubt." Julia nodded. "Oh, you poor dear. The subject, I would imagine, was Stephen. But are the rumors true?"

Julia related the story of the baker's wife and Stephen's night out. "So you see, something must be done."

"To save Stephen's business and your way of life, as well as to inflict a modicum of justice. Julia, you can't think clearly in this environment. Leave London for a while. Visit your parents. The fresh air and family consolation will clear your mind so you can properly cope."

"Their consolation will merely increase my anxiety and determination to not merely cope, but to rid myself of the problem. Your mother says it's impossible, but I must try. And I do not wish to saddle my family with the burden I carry."

"But what will you do? What can you do?"

"I will find a way. Meanwhile Stephen's behavior will be stanched. Your dear mother will see to it. Oh, I am so tired." And she fell back against the pillows.

"You must stay the night. You are in no condition to go home and face Stephen. After breakfast you will ride home in the carriage. I will send the driver with a message that you are fatigued and will return home tomorrow."

"You will do no such thing. A little unease on his part is justified. Thank you, dear Georgina for a respite for the night." And after hot milk and cocoa, for she wanted no more, her friend escorted her to the guest room and like a good mother put a child to bed.

Julia had a long and troubled sleep, but she awoke rested. Mornings were quiet in the Willie household. The children were at their lessons in the playroom. Robert had left early for work and Julia and Georgina were able to enjoy the toast, jam and tea in the morning room undisturbed.

"How do you manage, Georgina. Your married life is so happy and harmonious."

"I'm not as bright and capable as you, Julia. I flutter and fluff things often. It gives Robert something to do. He must right wrongs and fill in for my deficiencies. He's needed. I'm not a total fluff. I can manage on my own, but not all that well. Robert is never sure what mishap I may create next. You could say his marriage to me is an adventure. You could manage on your own, if you had the money, of course, so Stephen looks for adventure elsewhere. I'm not urging you to act stupid and helpless. That good an actress, dear friend, you are not, nor should you have to be, but there it is. Some men wander, as A London Lady makes clear. The Prince Regent's escapades do not encourage me to believe that the situation will get better. He is not a role model for male restraint. I stand ready to help you in any way I can."

"I may devise something outrageous."

"No one will find my participation in such a scheme unusual."

"You are a treasure, Georgina. Meanwhile I have the happy distraction today of a mandolin lesson with Edward Riley. He's a splendid teacher, so kind and gentle with me."

"He's also a very handsome man, Julia. Be careful."

# CHAPTER EIGHT

"I'm so glad you enjoyed the concert, Lady Langley."

"Oh, yes. It encouraged me to practice more and reach for the moon in proficiency."

"You've already progressed splendidly, m'lady. Let me hear you play the opening bars of that Beethoven piece again."

Julia obliged, and Edward closed his eyes as he listened. "There is such sweetness in your playing."

"It's a simple melody," said Julia.

"Simple melodies are the most neglected. Their import is so often lost in mundane playing. Again, and continue to the end." So Julia played and Edward began to sing.

> Tell me, my darling, that you love me,
> tell me that you are mine,
> and I shall not envy the gods their divinity!
> With one single glance,
> darling, with a smile
> you open a paradise
> of happiness for me!

When the music ceased neither was able to speak a word. Marie, sitting in the corner, was likewise enthralled. Finally, Edward cleared his throat.

"Well done," he said hoarsely."

"With difficulty," responded Julia, "but I thank you."

The bell rope indicated that Marie was needed in the kitchen. She rose from her chair.

"Thank you," Julia called to her retreating figure.

"No, thank you, m'lady," she responded, as she turned a euphoric face to Lady Langley, bowed, and exited humming.

"Shall we proceed?" asked Edward softly, his voice cracking. The instruction advanced a step, but no more. "Perhaps this is enough for today."

"We've time still; the hour is not up. Perhaps a bit more?"

Edward seemed ill at ease. "Perhaps. Turn to page ten." He demonstrated the chords for the next selection in the book, and Julia mastered them quickly.

"This time you attempt the melody and I will play the base." So they did.

The music that sprang from their instruments was now louder, more assured, the pleasure to them both more obvious.

"We play well together" said Edward. "Let's continue to do so at each session. "

"Julia plays well enough now," came a voice from the door. Stephen Langley stood there stiffly, then entered the room. "Thank you for tutoring my wife so well. There will be no need for further instruction or playing together. Wait in the entry hall, Mr. Riley. I will be there shortly to pay you for your service."

Edward Riley bowed to the master of the house and his lady and left the library.

"What else have you been playing at, Julia?"

"Stephen!"

"What other service has young Riley rendered?"

"How dare you speak to me so!"

"While I am hard at work in the office, I expect my wife to be equally so at home, even when she's attempting to gain musical ability. Music is an art of the highest order, meant to please the mind, and shake the cares of the day, not to pleasure other parts of the anatomy."

"Marie was here all this hour and only left five minutes ago to attend to a kitchen matter."

"A lot can happen in five minutes."

"But nothing did, except the music that you heard."

"I hope this is so."

"If you are uncertain you can expunge all doubt by giving me a divorce."

Stephen Langley's voice softened and his face relaxed. "I'm sorry, dear. What was I to think? Only two of you in the room and in such close proximity."

"If you trusted me you would think honorably of me and my instructor. You would be proud to have an ability in your wife to show off to your friends and business associates."

"That's unfair, Julia. I only agreed to have you learn to play the mandolin for your own pleasure. I'm sorry I've upset you. Think no more of it."

"Then the lessons may continue?"

"No, Mr. Riley is neglecting his duty to Lord Tilton to accommodate your interest in the mandolin."

"Has Lord Tilton said so?"

"Not exactly. I inferred it from our chats."

"Have it your way, Stephen. You are the master of this house," she said with resignation.

He kissed her lightly on the cheek. "Forgive me." and he left the library.

"But not the master of me," Julia whispered softly, as she gazed unseeing out the dining room window, at London going about its closing day affairs.

*******

"He's jealous! Wonderful! That may put a crimp in his nighttime affairs."

"A crimp, perhaps, Aunt Margaret, but not a stop. I've lived in London long enough to understand that those engaged in nefarious activities assume that others do the same, that their behavior is normal. But heaven forbid their wives should emulate their behavior. Sexual freedom is a one-way street."

"So true, my dear, but men do shoulder burdens we do not. Our personal financial upkeep and that of the household and the nation is theirs. We are relieved of this responsibility."

"The tradeoff is imposed on us. And being responsible in one area of life does not entitle them to be irresponsible in another."

"True, dear, but to be realistic we must acknowledge that some men feel that a sexual entitlement accompanies an elevated social position."

"Acknowledged but not accepted."

"Arguing the fact won't change it, Julia." And she poured herself another cup of tea. A nice cup of tea was the solution to all that was insoluble.

******

Lady Willie waited until the waiter had left after pouring their second cup of coffee before continuing their conversation.

"But Julia, you know nothing about him. Appearances can be deceiving, and I'm sure he doesn't need your help for anything. He is employed by one of the wealthiest men in England, who can do more for him than you can."

"I feel badly for him. He was all but accused of being a blackguard. Something should be done to rectify the mistake and make it up to him."

"That's for Stephen to do if he wishes, and it doesn't seem that he wishes. I'm sure that Edward has suffered similar indignities at other times. His looks must be a daunting obstacle to overcome, and other husbands have no doubt come to similar conclusions."

"Well, it isn't fair."

"We're in London, darling, you talk of being fair?"

"I could ask Lord Tilton for advice."

"He apparently knows no more about Edward than you do. He told my Robert that Edward was recommended for the position by Lord Kendall himself who was closing the mansion for the season to visit friends in France."

"Did he tell Lord Tilton nothing about Edward?"

"They didn't communicate in person. Lord Kendall made the recommendation in a letter of thanks for Lord Tilton's congratulatory note on his ascension to his father's fortune and estate. Lord Tilton knew his father well, they were boyhood friends, but he only met the son as a toddler."

"How did Gerald come to speak to Robert about this?"

"Robert has been advising Lord Tilton on lady's fabrics. Yes, Julia, laugh if you will, but Lord Tilton has ordered luxurious fabrics to present to Amy Burton as a gift."

"A man doesn't do such things!"

"Lord Tilton does. He's besotted with Amy and hopes to indicate what she can look forward to as his wife. He means to counter the belief that he's stingy. At least he didn't purchase undergarments. And he's contracted with our favorite dressmaker to design the garments to her taste."

"If she wears the clothes created from the fabrics he'll know he's won her, but that isn't likely to be soon. She seems to be enjoying her widowhood a great deal. But you think I should let the matter with Edward rest?"

"Yes. He's given you the gift of music and you've given him your thanks. Let that be the end of it."

# CHAPTER NINE

But the end of it seemed not to be in sight. The next day was Julia's market day, and she was filling her basket with nuncheon treats when a voice behind her said "Hello. May I walk with you?" Her market garb was simple and her basket almost full. "Of course," she replied. A new vendor on the street was offering unusual-looking crumpets with exotic fruits jettisoning out at irregular intervals. Julia dropped two into the rustic sack and moved on. Edward Riley pointed to their bench in the distance, but arrested her movement toward it with a restraining hand on her shoulder, as he stopped for two pints of ale from another new vendor. They reached the bench in silence. Edward retrieved two cups from his knapsack and poured some of the libation into each. They raised their cups in a toast and downed the spirits.

Julia shuddered. "Strong," she exclaimed, "and bitter. Not at all like the ale I shared with my father at day's end."

"I'm sorry. Sometimes experiments don't work out. Does your crumpet pass the test?"

Julia took a bite and smiled and followed the morsel with her milder brew.

"I'm sorry our lessons have ended, but you know enough to continue on your own."

"I'm sorry they ended as they did. My husband didn't understand. I made the matter clear to him and he regrets his ill-conceived words to you."

"A superficial regret, Lady Langley, or our lessons would continue. But let us speak no more of that."

Julia offered him a crumpet. He accepted. "A more digestible form of regret than your husband's words." They ate and drank silently, Julia's eyes fixed on the passing crowd and Edward's fixed on her.

"I will be going home soon. I must help festoon the mansion for the Christmas festivities. The family must be entertained and the staff is honored at Christmas as well."

"How extraordinary!"

"Yes, and most appreciated. We have a long list of applicants for service at the mansion. I am sure that the wages we pay, which are the highest in the county, have some bearing on the desire to work for us."

"Is the family gathering a large one?"

"Alas, no. Lord Kendall was his father's only son, and since he remains unmarried, no wife or children exist to enjoy the occasion or cheer the distant relatives who do attend."

"They have no relatives or family of their own?"

"They do, but those who grace the mansion with their presence are not as welcome with their closer kin. They are the black sheep of their families. Cousin Reginald is a devout Whig, and politics his favorite food for conversation. He detests the Prince of Wales. Uncle Edgar, however, is as vociferous in his praise of the Regent as Reginald is in his castigation of him. Uncle Edgar, you see, is a poet and essayist of local renown, and since the Regent is a patron of the arts, he can do no wrong in Edgar's eyes. He wife, Aunt Dorothea, is silent during his verbal effusions, but nods her agreement periodically. Reginald and Edgar would in happier times go to the same family celebrations, but their hosts have ceased inviting them and begged my Lord's father to do so as a great favor to preserve their sanity. The current Lord continues his father's kindness. Fortunately we have Cousin Wilbur as peacemaker. He's a kindly old bachelor who would be welcome anywhere, but who chooses to hone his negotiating skills annually at our Christmas table."

"What a fascinating family! I'd enjoy meeting them."

"You would have a warming and wondrous effect on them all. Cousin Wilbur would appreciate a helping hand."

"Will your master resume his studies at Oxford in the new year?"

"No, they were advanced studies and they have been concluded. He returns home with his love of history and culture intact and with the resources of our vast library to satisfy further learning desires as he devotes more time to the estate."

"My parents knew his father well. His estate is less than a day's journey from our own. Since my marriage he has visited my family a half dozen times and engaged in a voluminous correspondence with my father, whose agricultural success is due in part to the guidance given by Lord Kendall. Is the son as kind and generous?"

"The son is much like the father. Will you be visiting your parents over Christmas?"

"Yes. You think that we can join Cousin Wilbur and outnumber the adversaries to create a semblance of peace?"

"I think you can do more than that. And from what I've heard your parents have spirituality running through their veins, a most important attribute for any time, but especially for this holiest and happiest of holidays. Is there any chance that your husband could contribute peaceful tidings as well?"

Julia laughed. "There is always a chance. If talk turns to estate life the chances are dimmed. My father is well aware of this and never discusses estate matters in his presence."

"It weighs heavily on him, then, that he is a second son?"

"It shouldn't, but it does. Inheritance is lovely, there's no denying that, but he can be proud of what he has achieved."

"With the help of his wife, I have heard."

"Tired gossip. I have done nothing."

"Sometimes doing is less important than being. I've heard nothing but accolades in that department. When I ask about Stephen, the response is about you."

"Why have you been asking about Stephen?"

"Curiosity about who Lord Langley does business with."

"Are you truly a handyman at the Kendall estate?"

"My work comes in handy."

"Very amusing. Has Lord Tilton hired you to amuse him or to do actual work?"

"A reprimand well taken, Lady Langley. I have been untruthful about my curiosity about your husband. Would you like to know why I've inquired about him?"

"No. I must be going. A journeyman will be arriving soon to examine the roof. The leak was repaired, but not well. It continues to soak through the maid's ceiling."

"Perhaps the tar was not sufficiently applied."

"Perhaps."

"You can tar and tile. Tile would look well."

"Have you priced tiles lately?"

"Lord Langley does not wish to bear the expense?"

Julia rose, noted once more the lateness of the hour and said her goodbye, resisting the strong temptation to tell Edward Riley that her husband's expenditures and wishes were none of his business.

The young man looked after her as she strode off. His school studies had taught him much, but not how to use diplomacy in addressing the married woman he loved.

******

"Yes, Georgina, I relive my happy, uncomplicated childhood weekly as best I can by a trip to the country markets near Mount Street. I've enjoyed them so, but how can I continue while Edward Riley is in London? It can't be a coincidence that he's there when I'm there. He's pleasant enough, but too inquisitive. My personal life is not to be shared with someone I barely know and whose interest in a married woman is presumptuous."

"It is flattering. He's a decent man from all accounts. I've discreetly inquired of Lord Tilton and he'll be gone by the new year, so what's the harm in being in the company of an attractive man whose interests parallel yours, in broad daylight in a part of the city where a titled lady would be inconspicuous?"

"You told me to beware of him."

"That was before I knew he was a decent sort. Why shouldn't you safely enjoy his admiration and his conversation?"

"The safety may be an illusion. I hardly consider Lord Tilton, who is a darling, an expert on maneuvers concerning affairs of the heart. Amy Burton's behavior has him bewildered and disconcerted beyond belief. You would think he had never been a suitor before."

"It's been a long time, and many things in London and elsewhere have changed."

"And what was once deemed unthinkable is now acceptable in business and in married life."

"The poor man is indeed befuddled. His weekly correspondence to me is filled with anguished questions I am at a loss to answer. Consolation and fortitude is the most I can offer."

"Weekly correspondence? His footman delivers messages to me almost daily. I don't want to encourage Edward Riley in his pursuit of me, but I do wish I could assist Lord Tilton in his pursuit of Amy Burton."

"They are so different." Georgina sighed.

"But he's in love."

Georgina nodded. "Hopelessly."

"It may yet work out. She hasn't yet chosen a husband, and seems to dispense equal favor to her suitors."

"Not the one favor they seek, I believe."

"I think, if she intends to marry at all, she will choose the man, in this bawdy town, who desires her for herself, beyond that essential favor, Georgina."

"Then Lord Tilton has a chance. He's besotted with more than her outward person."

"Astrologers try not to disillusion him, he pays well, but their differences are obvious, in life as well as in their charts. Yes, he's been to astrologers."

"So you must dream up comfort for him more than I. He presses you more for guidance, I think, because he actively pursues business with Stephen, his land holdings are so widespread, and he sees you both more often for social as well as business reasons. Also, and I hesitated to say this Julia, but I believe he seeks guidance from a kindred spirit, one whose marriage complications echo his own."

"Is the gossip so widespread?"

"It's been growing lately. Lord Tilton must cope with a woman with many suitors, and you must cope with a man with a wandering eye."

"So the gossip does not include the belief that other parts of his anatomy wander?"

"People are loathe to believe that such a beautiful, kind and caring woman as yourself could be so misused."

"But this is London, and the belief no doubt exists."

"Stephen was deprived of an inheritance. He was born too late. He may be seeking to make up for that loss by enjoying favors in another area. Gossip that has reached my ears concerns his interest in women married to men of substance, mainly inherited substance. The losses incurred in both are often hard to overcome. There is something to pity in that."

"Would you pity him if her were your husband?"

"I'd crack a chair over his head, for starters."

"Your Robert is a second son, but a faithful husband."

"Different men react differently."

"Your mother is working to discover the main objects of Stephen's interest. Then we will discuss how to curb his appetite for them."

"Mother has told me. But she believes the appetite is merely physical, that he loves only you."

"To him it may be 'merely.' What would follow a chair over the head?"

"All the chairs in the room!"

"The design of my dear aunt, your mother, is to remove his access to the objects he consorts with, and after reducing their availability, make him jealous of the attention other men give me."

"Edward Riley! Make the most of him before he leaves."

"Georgina, I'd be as bad as Stephen if I used Edward Riley to forward this scheme."

"He can't have you, he must know that, so any signs of affection you confer on him would be appreciated. He can leave with memories to cherish, a fairy tale love, beautiful, rewarded, though ultimately unrequited."

"I'd feel so guilty using our friendship this way."

"Ah, so you have a friendship."

"We've enjoyed our music lesson chats, our market day walks, our nuncheon treats, a sort of friendship, yes, not intimate, not personal, but I'd be using him and abusing my marriage vows."

"Do you want to set your marriage to rights or do you not? You can put on a saintly, martyred cloak or do what you must to make the rest of your life at least palatable. And Stephen wants children. He's told Robert he's embarrassed to respond to questions about why, after five years, he has none. Men are questioning his manliness, not your ability to produce. You refuse to have a child with him in his present wayward condition. This can't go on. Your marriage will worsen and your unhappiness will increase. Mother is right. Reduce Stephen's access to women and increase his jealousy of men's access to you — a two-pronged attack. Go for it Julia. Have you another solution in mind?"

Julia bit her lip. "No."

## CHAPTER TEN

Julia hesitated to go for her stroll and nuncheon the following week. Her purpose, if she did, would be both laudable and nefarious. The situation that might lead to her happiness would lead to the unhappiness of someone she liked, but need it do so? She could go and enjoy the outing and company and make it clear to Edward that their meetings were held in friendship, nothing more. If he chose to interpret them as something more she had no control over that. She would be open and honest, and soon he would be gone. It seemed the days flew by and market day was upon her. Had they flown because she was busy with mundane household chores, or because she was already living in the present. No matter. She would not carry a basket this day. She would simply eat, drink, chat — and run! As Julia moved among the vendors she saw no sign of Edward, but relief turned to dismay as she approached the bench they had shared. It was occupied by Edward holding a bunch of daisies, which he gave her as she joined him.

"Please accept this simple meadowland bouquet as my apology for offending you. Do speak to me."

"Thank you. I'll speak."

"Good, because I am anxious to hear your opinion of the exhibit at Somerset House, if you've seen it."

"No, I haven't, but I've been meaning to. Nature is depicted and the results so variously interpreted that I've been anxious to see for myself what the controversy is about. I do miss the countryside of my youth, my own art reflects it, and seeing it in paint and watercolor and colored pencil is better than not seeing it at all, except for my annual visit to my parents."

A vendor passed near shouting "Chestnuts! Hot chestnuts!" spreading aroma and smoke to all nearby. Julia coughed and laughed. "Fresh air would be very welcome in London, even if only to be enjoyed on canvas."

"Oh, we must see the exhibit! I, too, long for the countryside. Wait!"

Edward jumped up and with a few long strides was at the chestnut vendor's cart. He returned with a bag filled with aromatic fragrance sans smoke. "This will go well with the apple cider we've bought. In liquids we seem to think alike, perhaps in art, too? If you can spare the time, will you join me in a stroll to Somerset House to see what the Royal Academy of Fine Arts has wrought?"

Julia thought, "Heavens, no!" but the words she spoke were "I would enjoy that."

So they ate, drank, smiled and proceeded to Somerset House. Along the way Julia divested herself of the flowers. One was given to a little girl with a yellow pinwheel to match, two others to a sour-faced, middle-aged woman walking quickly to a waiting sullen man, and three to an elderly woman slowly ascending the stairs of a timeworn residence. Somerset House was not crowded. They could view the paintings in comfort, as could the paintings view them. What the paintings thought of the young couple they did not say, but the couple's views of them were complementary. Edward saw the realism of the blades of grass, the trees. Julia saw the impressionistic soul of living nature, both what the eyes saw and the heart felt, both conclusions sometimes drawn from the same paintings.

"Will you accept some hot tea, so we can continue discussing the various charms adorning the Somerset House walls?"

Indeed she would, but Julia blanched when she saw the establishment he chose to enter was Gunter's. Their renowned pastries were expensive, and the Naples Divoline he urged upon her was even more so. Their chat would cost him dearly. But there they were and he was charmingly persuasive. With a sharp intake of breath she realized their rendezvous would be reported to her social set. At the counter making purchases were the Duchess of Marlborough's maid and the Baroness Kent's housekeeper. Had Edward purposely chosen this patisserie to announce to the world his interest in Lord Langley's wife? It would be pointless to complain to Lady Brighton or Georgina. They would be as one in their approval. Edward parted from her a block before they reached her residence. At least he had the sense not to see her to her door, which she would not have allowed even had he asked to do so. At home Julia strode the length of the library for fifteen minutes, both berating and congratulating herself on the progress she had made that day forwarding the plans of her co-conspirators who intended through stealth and deceit to achieve the noble goal of freeing her from enduring the immoral activities of her lascivious and respected husband. She sat at the library table and wrote to her friends and demons: "Nuncheon with Edward as usual. Art exhibit at The Royal Academy. Tea and sweets at Gunter's. Seen by servants of the ton. Hope you're satisfied."

She rang for Reggie to deliver the missives to both women. Then she searched the library for art books that would illuminate the methods and history of the works she and Edward had viewed that day.

Julia was now seeing Edward Riley more frequently. They conversed on strolls through Vauxhall Gardens, past the fountains, statues and artificial ruins, enjoying the gardens. When Stephen told her that evening "work" would keep him at the office, she chose to spend them with Edward at the Gardens' supper boxes lit by thousands of lanterns that hung from the cast iron pillars of the vaulted colonnade, enjoying the musical entertainment that in earlier days she had enjoyed with Stephen, whose entertainment excursions now centered around culture with a profitable element. Entertainments at Drury Lane and Covent Garden masked a desired visibility to an elite clientele who might need assistance from Lord Langley and his bank. But now, strolling through Hyde Park, Edward was proposing an evening at one of Stephen's haunts.

"I adore Mozart, Edward, but a night at Covent Garden should be spent with my husband. Our friendship has already set tongues to wagging. We need not give the gossips more to report."

"But THE MARRIAGE OF FIGARO is such a delightful opera. Naturally, you should offer your husband first right of refusal, but if he refuses there can surely be no reason for you to deprive yourself of an evening with the great master."

Julia raised her eyebrows.

"I mean Mozart, not me." Edward laughed.

"You assume a wife has more privileges than she actually possesses. Stephen must agree to my evening with you in such a formal setting, and I doubt that he would. People will conjecture the worst fantasies. And they will assume that Stephen's interests lay in areas other than in pleasing his wife."

"Do they not?"

"I am a married woman and you are a friend, that is all. That is a lot, and it is precious to me, but that is all. Surely you realize it can be no other way."

"What if it could be?"

"It cannot be. Please, I'm tired. I must be leaving now." She pressed his hand in friendship, turned and walked away.

Edward stood silently, watching her disappear down the street. It was a long walk to Lord Tilton's mansion, but he walked, unseeing, down the crowded street, bumping into people, nearly upsetting a pushcart that appeared out of nowhere, and mindless of the drizzle that soon began to fall.

# CHAPTER ELEVEN

Julia was grateful it was Thursday. She had been considering her emotional woes all week. Now she would be considering and catering to the real needs of others. She assembled the gifts for her weekly hospital visit to the wounded military. She filled her basket with the pastries she herself had baked that morning and assorted chocolates imported from Denmark, treats that differed from the week before. The men enjoyed the pastry surprises and the personal effort involved in selecting and producing them. A carriage ride to the wounded navy occupants of Ward 11 at Bartholomews Hospital would be an affront to Julia's sense of propriety. She walked. She was not aware that the walk brought a becoming blush to her cheeks and that this as well as her cheerful company lifted the men's spirits. The gifts were welcome, but mattered less. Lady Langley was greeted with a welcoming ballad the men had created just for her, not sung too badly by the eight occupants of the ward.

"What have you been up to all week?" And they eagerly responded. The "up to" had been figurative, since half the men were on crutches. Julia was as eager to speak to them as they to her. They had been wounded as they engaged in combat with Napoleon's navy. Her brother Jonathan, they knew, had done the same, fighting to defeat the despot. The news that the British navy had succeeded was several months old, but the fighting the men had engaged in was still fresh in their minds. The army had engaged in face-to-face combat, but without naval support could not have succeeded. Julia heard fresh tales of stealth attacks on ships at midnight, of boarding vessels and acquiring enemy supplies, of dispatching their adversaries with planks, bottles and fire. They glowed with pride as they recounted the exploits of the British navy, and Julia listened with awe and appreciation for the sacrifices and dangers they endured that brought victory for the British cause. But Julia reflected that war, even a just war, was a sad thing. The French soldiers fighting the British were husbands, sons, fathers, too. Whether they believed in their cause she could not know, but they were required by their profession to put their lives and the lives of others at risk. She was glad the men sitting and standing before her had survived, but at what cost to themselves and others. As she listened she remembered the similar excitement her brother Jonathan had shown anticipating his entry into the British navy. She was a mere fifteen, and he a strapping fellow of twenty-five. Neither tending crops nor caring for the animals thrilled him. He couldn't sit still, he had constantly to be moving, and he had signed up as soon as he could. He had done well. His parents had sent her his last letter. It read — "We are victorious! The French tyrant has been defeated, and those of us who ventured beyond our duty have been rewarded. I am now admiral of our fleet! I have two weeks to visit you to enjoy your warmth and love, and then to Julia, my darling sister, whom I've missed as much as I've missed you. Tell her she has had a heroic part in our enterprise. A picture of her, which I carry with me always, has uplifted the spirits and softened the blows of exhaustion and exertion we've encountered. I posted it where all could see and profit from it, and were she not already married, she could have her pick of every unmarried man on the ship. I anxiously await seeing you all again. My boundless love to you and her."

******

"Oh Julia, what a time you shall have preparing for his visit, but what a wonderful time! Your dining area can only hold so many. How will you decide whom to invite? All of London will want to have dinner with a hero of the war." The hour was late, and the cafe nearly empty.

"Well, we thought, Georgina, that a small intimate party of friends would be best, The mayor will greet Admiral Geffen upon his arrival, and he will visit our injured military. Otherwise, his visit is a personal one."

"'We thought' sounds like Stephen, not like you. Can't you persuade him otherwise?"

"If I could have I would have. When a man once experiences poverty he does not forget it. You know how costs are rising. I'm continually asking him for increases in the household budget."

"We all are, but even without the cushion of inherited wealth, he does have a secure, well-paying position at the bank."

Julia shook her head. "Tell him that. Jonathan will appreciate an interlude from public adoration. His visit is, after all, to see me."

"Of course. I hope Robert and I are invited."

"You know you are. I wouldn't dream of omitting my dearest friend who is the sister I never had. I'm preparing the guest list now. You can imagine the reason most will be invited, even if not their names."

"Friends of Stephen, no doubt, whose bank accounts warrant their inclusion. Really, Julia, his actions are so predictable and so tiresome. But I don't mean to upset you. At least no women will be there alone to distract Jonathan from you. He is a handsome man, probably besieged by women when he is not in battle."

Julia laughed. "Very much so, and his letters indicate that he enjoys their attention immensely."

"Any sister-in-law on the horizon?"

"Not yet. My parents are clamoring for grandchildren, and since I have not obliged, their hopes rest on Jonathan."

"I wonder why Edward Riley has not seen service."

"Have pity on the women, Georgina. If eligible men are not available to our sex for companionship at the very least, our lives would be the lesser for it. We've lost so many in the war."

"Lord Tilton has said that he makes extensive use of the mansion library. His interests seem to lie in history and the arts. If Lord Tilton knows more about him he isn't saying. I've asked. The handsome estate worker is a bit of a mystery."

"We're all entitled to privacy, Georgina. The whole world need not know our background or our goals."

"True, but when an unmarried, handsome man is interested in a married woman who is my best friend, more knowledge about him would put my mind at ease —or not. Haven't you wondered about him at all?"

"A bit, but I'm busy with my own life. Thank you, dear friend for your concern, but I'm in no danger. The music lessons are over and we meet in passing on the street and chat. Has Lord Tilton said he has spoken of me?"

Georgina hesitated. "No, but why should he mention a servant at all? And he mentions him frequently, even in the midst of discussions about fabric to adorn Amy Burton. Robert is puzzled too."

"Lord Tilton has no children. That blessing was denied him and his late wife. He has no immediate heir. Perhaps he is thinking of adopting one. Heirless men have been known to adopt men in their twenties or older to carry on the family name."

"Perhaps, but I would like to know for certain, if that is the case. I've a mind to ask Robert to ask Lord Tilton."

"I would be pleased to convey any message you have for him, orally or in writing, if privacy is paramount."

The women looked up from their tea. The offer came from Edward Riley.

"May I be seated or would I be intruding?" He seated himself before receiving a response. "I've been looking for you, Lady

Langley. I was told by your butler that you and Lady Willie were exploring the shops, so I've been searching the streets for you. I assumed you would stop for a spot of tea. Lord Tilton was hoping you would allow him a visit this evening on a matter of personal importance. I only speak before Lady Willie of this because Lord Willie has provided the fabrics that relate to the lady that relates to this matter."

"I would be happy to oblige my friend Lord Tilton. Would eight o'clock be convenient for his lordship? if so, he can join us for dinner."

"That is most kind of you, Lady Langley, but his lordship does not wish to mix his desire for privacy and guidance with the conviviality associated with dinner. Perhaps six o'clock would be convenient for you?"

"Yes, I'll see Lord Tilton with pleasure. Lord Langley will be home later. Six o'clock, then, for a private talk for just the two of us."

"Is there a message you wanted me to convey to Lord Tilton, Lady Willie?"

"No, none at all," said Georgina, looking away to hide a blush.

"Well, then, I won't interrupt your tea any longer." He stood and hesitated, as if waiting for an invitation to linger, before tipping his hat and walking off.

"How much longer will he remain in London, Julia?" Her friend shook her head. "Do ask Lord Tilton. I wish you would also ask if Edward Riley is making any female friends in London or at the estate or anywhere."

"I'll do my best to allay your fears. I have none. Now we must both be off to complete our tasks. The milliner awaits you and the house awaits me. The hour is late."

"Come with me, Julia. I would like your opinion on the bonnets I am considering. Then you can ride home in the carriage."

"A walk will do me good."

Georgina looked at her friend's feet. "You're wearing out more shoes in a month than anyone I know."

"Stephen says our carriage has seen too much use lately. The cost of repairs edges ever higher."

"He uses the carriage more than you. The blame, if any, should be borne by him. But your shoes are worn by you alone and are costly as well. Come with me and then ride home."

Julia smiled. "I'm persuaded, and I would like a preview of your new chapeau."

******

When Lord Tilton arrived Julia escorted him to the library, where she herself had laid the cloth on the table, and the sweets she knew he fancied and the tea piping hot upon a crested plate.

"My dear friend, have some tea and pastry before you speak. Then, after you have dispelled that anxious look and relaxed tell me how I can help you." She followed the suggestion she had given him, smiled warmly, put down her teacup and waited.

"I want to gift Amy with a frock of elegant fabric, and I don't know what would please her. You've spoken with her, seen what she wears and know the latest styles. What would you suggest?"

"You don't want to gift her the cloth and have it made up in the usual way?"

"No, I want to gift her with a fully made frock. She should have no cause to spend money completing it."

"You could present her with the fabric and tell her you have instructed Jeremy and Taylor to charge you the amount for transforming it into a dress of her choosing, they do best with such fabrics."

"I could, but wouldn't a full completed frock be a more awesome gift? Otherwise it's like a puzzle whose complete picture is only seen after bits and pieces are put together."

"Bits and pieces is the usual way, and the safer one. You can then be assured the result will be to her liking."

"I have her measurements; she's bought from Robert before. But you think the usual is the better way?"

"Yes, that's why it's usual. A work in progress can be altered on its way to completion, a finished product cannot. What fabric have you chosen?"

"They are in the plural: pink silk, lavender satin, white organdy. I wanted the most luxurious for the body and the decoration."

"Heavens, how much fabric did you buy?"

"Robert thinks it's enough for two or three garments, but this way, you see, she wouldn't fear having at least enough for one, and she can save the rest for future use. I want her to be happy."

"She should be ecstatic! These are not daytime fabrics. Do you anticipate her going to musicals, operas, balls frequently?"

"Yes, with me. I hope, I wish, oh, Julia, I don't know! Am I expecting too much from one gift?"

"Will she have a birthday soon?"

"No, must she?"

"Bombarding her with so much at once may make you seem desperate to win her affection."

"I am."

"Dear Gerald, parcel out your love in smaller doses. Jeremy and Taylor have a backlog of work so the gift will not metamorphose into dresses immediately. I myself am on their waiting list, so give your gift in three parts. Three female saints days will soon be upon us. Gift the fabrics on those occasions. Done this way your gifts will be three instead of one and demonstrate your holy commitment to her and to the saints. Your meaning will be elevated above desperation."

"Thank you, Julia. You are a godsend. Is there anything I can do for you?"

"No, dear Gerald. You have already. My performance on the mandolin is quite tolerable, thanks to the instructor you sent me."

"I'm glad. I regret your duties did not permit you to continue with the lessons. Stephen told me."

"Did he. Will Mr. Riley be with you much longer?"

"Several more weeks. He will be happy to hear his instructions have borne fruit. He often asks about you."

"What prompted you to select him as temporary handyman?"

"His master's father and I were school mates, and he praised Edward often for his work."

"Has he a family of his own?"

"None that is immediate."

"Has he a goal beyond his current trade?"

"He has many interests and he is a cultured man. The path he ultimately chooses will to a large degree be affected by the wife he chooses. He is much sought after, but he is cautious. A wife, a profession are major steps requiring serious reflection."

"Is any of his education formal?"

"He chooses not to have that known. But he does have heartfelt interests he can choose to follow. Sometimes heartfelt desires can lead one astray. Desires of the heart should meet the approval of the head if they are to run a successful course."

"Your profession was expected of you, Gerald, did your head approve?"

"Yes, I had the good fortune to approve my lot in life."

"And was your choice of wife determined in the same way?"

"Indeed, both my head and my heart approved the happy choice."

"Did your head approve your heart's choice, or did your heart approve your head's choice?"

"Both approved at the same time."

"Then you were fortunate indeed."

Lord Tilton shifted awkwardly in his chair. "Thank you for your guidance in my gift-giving quandry. I hope that Amy's heart, to continue the analogy, will appreciate the fabric, and that her head will appreciate me."

"Are you out to win her head or her heart?"

"Both, in whatever way and whatever proportion I can."

"Your success in doing so is in my prayers."

Lord Tilton took his leave, and after Julia closed the door, she leaned against it for a moment. When affairs of the heart must meet the approval of the head happiness can never be complete. Is it not for the head, whether it approves or not, she pondered, to make the heart's choice workable? She wondered how Amy Burton was dealing with the heart-head dilemma, if one even existed for her. How Stephen rationalized his head/heart choices she did not know. But she knew her own heart. As for her head, she knew enough to keep it out of her heart's range. She disliked fighting. But to give her heart its contemplative due, it did recognize that 40, 50, 60 years was a long time to be unhappy.

# CHAPTER TWELVE

Julia read the card with astonishment:

In celebration of the six weeks you have pursued excellence in playing the mandolin.
From our Kendall estate.<br>Edward Riley

She had opened the door to retrieve the newspaper, and there they were - the card and a huge bouquet of pink and white blossoms that blocked the door and the newspaper beyond it. They spread their glory from a farmer's milk can, which revived happy memories of younger days and earlier work. She carried the gift to her bedchamber and placed it in a sunny window spot. It was a kind and thoughtful gift, and an embarrassing one, not a broad spray of colors but a spray symbolizing purity and femininity and a homespun elegance. And they were not storebought impersonal messengers, but came from the estate he called home. Their significance was clear and unwelcome. What did he want of her? They could only be friends, and distant ones at that.

"It's an infatuation," she said, "and it will pass."

Julia rose an hour before Stephen to spend that precious time before their breakfast reading the newspaper and communing with the world in the privacy of her bedchamber. A newspaper subscription was costly, and Stephen chose THE TIMES, which focused on verified news of London and abroad, omitting gossip, theory and flights of imagination. This was fine with Julia. It was a precious connection to life beyond the four walls, and it could only be accessed before Stephen read it at the breakfast table and carried it away with him to the office. A distant request that he leave it with her he found laughable. What would she need it for? The news this morning was especially rewarding. Brother Jonathan's ship was moored in Marseilles and the paper contained his interview with a reporter. He praised his shipmates, recounting stories of their heroism and gloried in the British success in defeating Napoleon. He was humbled, he said, with his promotion to admiral. Julia lingered long over the interview before moving on to accounts of the rising cost of food and fuel, along with the monetary crisis and Parliament's struggle with a cash imbalance. Workers were striking for wages that would allow them to live in modest comfort. An influx of visitors looking for work in London was hampering their cause as well as straining the city's housing accommodations. There were advertisements for new goods, "just arrived" from the Continent — bonnets, frocks, stockings in the latest styles — which only some could afford. Stephen's bank had its usual advertisement. And Covent Garden was performing The Marriage of Figaro the following week. Both she and Stephen enjoyed Mozart operas, but two years into their marriage he began refusing to attend this one. Julia sighed. Infidelity ranked high in Figaro. Chastised by Mozart. Who could bear it? Julia brought the newspaper downstairs and left it next to Stephen's plate. She placed a few of the flowers she had received in an empty vase in the foyer and brought it to the dining room table. Marie had forgotten to purchase a morning display.

"Good morning, Julia." Stephen pecked her on the cheek. "Not our usual floral display, rather sparse. We can afford a bit more of nature to start the day.".

"They arrived from Lord Tilton's mansion."

"Ah, a thank you for your assistance in his romantic venture. With all the time you've devoted to his problem I would have expected a larger bouquet."

"It was larger. I reserved the rest for my bedchamber."

"A reasonable location. Would that Lord Tilton were more practical in his pursuit of the widow. In our investment discussions he keeps interjecting concerns about what she would like. A cottage in the lake district might suit her more than the interest on bonds, a Parisian wardrobe more than a mining company. Have you ever heard such nonsense? A man of sense and values has turned into a lovesick schoolboy. Naturally you have to help him, he's one of my most valued clients, but can you try to release him from this fixation on Amy Burton? She's a fine woman, but well able to take care of herself and provide any luxuries she desires. She would do well to provide for her future by investing the Burton inheritance, instead of leading a susceptible man astray with a demand for frivolities."

"She hasn't demanded, or even asked."

"As some men get older they behave foolishly. Mrs. Burton, however, seems to have all her faculties intact. I'm surprised she hasn't moved her investment portfolio into more productive hands than those of Wilson & Scott. Do you see much of her in a social way?"

"No, she doesn't seem to have time to socialize with women. Her male friends keep her quite busy."

"A woman should have female friends. You should attempt a better acquaintance."

"Is her investment portfolio that large?"

"Very large. I daresay your household budget could use another increase."

"Why attempt to snare her inheritance and disparage poor Lord Tilton's attachment to her when their marriage would mean her inheritance would become his and therefore yours to invest?"

"That's true, but she's an independent woman and, I surmise, a clever one and not likely to be caught by him or any man. The privilege of investing her funds is more safely assured if she is persuaded to invest them now, with me of course. I would gain a valuable client and you would gain a good friend."

"You have no fear that my learning from a clever woman would not redound to your benefit?"

Stephen laughed. "No, darling. I know you too well. She may be clever, but you are intelligent, and you know where your duty and benefit lie. Your brother is front page news. How wonderful! I look forward to meeting him again. Seven years is a long time to be absent from your relations. I'll soon have the guest list for our dinner honoring him. My clients are all clamoring to be invited, but as I told you we must be selective. Our home is sufficiently large for us and one or two children, should you decide to honor me with the title of father, but it is no mansion, so the whole world cannot be accommodated at this most wonderful event. Of course he comes to see you. All others are appendages to his desire to reunite with his sister. He really must do this more often."

Julia smiled in response. She and Stephen visited his father and brother annually out of duty, she, likewise, her parents, but out of love. Her mother usually visited her as well each autumn, but complications related to crop expansion kept her beside her husband this year. Still, letters flew between them as fast as the post would allow, the cost of paper be damned.

Stephen folded the newspaper and downed the last of the tea. "I'll be late tonight dear. If you are up when I return we'll share some tea, and with the usual peck on the cheek, he walked to the foyer where Jameson helped him on with his jacket and opened the door.

"Mrs. Burton! How delightful to see you! Julia was just speaking of you, lamenting that her acquaintance with you was so slight. You are most welcome!" And he walked down the steps and briskly down the street whistling.

Julia, alerted by his exclamation, was at the door to greet her guest. "Good morning, Mrs. Burton, but so early. Surely you haven't had breakfast. You must join me as I finish mine."

"Thank you, Lady Langley, I accept. I am fortified for this visit with orange juice only."

She followed Julia to the breakfast room where her hostess instructed Marie to assemble breakfast for her guest.

"Please dispense with Lady Langley. I am Julia. May I call you Amy?"

"Please do. I intrude without prior notice, but I could not resist. I had to talk to someone after receiving Lord Tilton's gift barely an hour ago, a gift I believe you are aware of but had no part in suggesting."

Julia sighed heavily. "Was your outrage so great?"

"No, dear, after the initial shock I was convulsed with laughter for at least five minutes. Whatever was he thinking!"

"He wasn't thinking. Two more sets of luxurious fabrics await you in the coming weeks. He was not to be dissuaded. The best I could do was to suggest that he not inundate you with them all at once."

"Does he see me as some Josephine or Marie Antoinette, primping and priming to bedazzle the world?"

"No, he sees you of such high estate that luxury becomes you."

"He hasn't seen me in curlers."

"It wouldn't matter. He sees you as a glamorous creature. What you place on your person will not change that. Do not repeat this, please, but Stephen told me that he wants his investments to revolve around pleasing you."

"And I thought he was a man of sense. His knowledge of investments is greater than mine."

"A wise wife can remind her husband of this, and marriage is his goal. I am not assuming it is yours. I only know Lord Tilton's heart, though it is hard to imagine that others do not know it too. I am responsible for the gifts appearing on three saints days. I hoped it would be perceived as elevating the worldly to the spiritual realm."

Amy laughed. "Good try, but I can imagine the saints wearing such apparel! I am sure they would do as I will. I will return the package. I would have sent it back with the messenger had I known its contents. I shall do the same with the next two arrivals should Gerald persist."

"Lord Tilton will be traumatized. He's a dear friend, but your reaction was understandable."

"Acceptance would signify obligation to wear the resulting clothes which would announce to all London a permanent relationship for which I am not prepared. I've long admired you Julia. Your disposition and character are evident at even a passing meeting. Your reputation as a charming, kind, intelligent woman is well earned, but it pertains to you as a singular person. With your husband along, you disappear. I cannot disappear. I will not disappear. As a widow I regained the freedom I had lost. I'm accorded slack in what I say and do because I take second place to no man. My husband was a cut above the usual. He treated me as an equal, even if society didn't, and he consulted me on a variety of matters requiring a decision. I appreciated that. I've considered you an admirable representative of our sex, limited only by your marital status, a status women have little choice but to attain, if they can. I have been troubled by rumors that you might be linked to a mischievous husband, that is what society would consider him to be, not the ungrateful, despicable excuse for a husband that wives would consider him to be. I hope the rumors are not true. Stories are often exaggerated beyond reality, but are painful for a wife to hear nonetheless. I am not inquiring into your personal life, heaven forbid. I only wish to say that if I can help in any way, should help be needed, I would be privileged to do so. Women should stick together, both the free and the incarcerated. We cannot change society, but we can make inroads in small, significant ways to rectify some of its egregious errors. A London Lady has done that, incognito, of course. Her life in London wouldn't be worth a farthing if her identity were known. Yes, small, but significant improvements are attainable goals, at least in our private lives."

"You are a dear, Amy Burton. I hope you will be able to attend the dinner we're having for my brother."

"I'd like to, but I cannot come with Lord Tilton. People will talk."

"They will talk anyway, especially in your absence."

They both laughed.

"What a pretty pass the social world has come to, and the political world no better," said Amy. "Or has it always been this way and, accepting it, we haven't noticed. But oh, Julia, I despair of women who play the victim and even more those who are the perpetrators of their own misfortunes. 'Where have I gone wrong,' they pout, 'I must be to blame.' "Amy laughed. "Yes, dear, I would be a handful for any man I marry because I will not be tethered or silenced, at least not much, and not without my consent. Of course men may feel likewise. Your brother is now the admiral of a fleet. If his military persona carries into his personal life he will be a handful for his wife as well. What is he like?"

"You shall judge for yourself at our banquet. You shall be invited whether you accompany Lord Tilton or not."

"A woman alone. I like that. I like that you will be shredding the rules. But I doubt that Stephen will approve, and even if you are inclined to do as you please he does pay the bills. My motto in carrying on as I do is 'Do No Harm,' and I fear harm would come of my attending without Lord Tilton as escort, and I cannot come with him. The tailors, servants will know of his gifts, spread the word faster than I can return them and assume the worst if I am seen with him before the fabrics are returned."

"You are coming. I do not accept your refusal. A small period of embarrassment does not faze a liberated woman who would surely criticize this excuse in anyone else."

Amy smiled, then laughed. "I accept your reprimand and your invitation!"

Cook herself now entered with scrambled eggs, bacon, red potatoes and fresh strawberries for Amy and a side platter more for the lady of the house, who winked at Mrs. North, who understood her ways, as breakfast was refreshed and enjoyed by both ladies.

\*\*\*\*\*\*

"Amy Burton will be invited, Stephen!" No, she would not say that. Amy will simply appear, her place card next to Jonathan's, to the dismay, no doubt, of all. Lady Brighton would enliven the other side of the table, flanked by the taciturn Lord Tilton, who would be forced to respond to her comments and queries, as everyone else always did. Like Amy Burton she too had a widow's freedom, and an imperious manner as well, approaching gall. She was respected and sometime feared, but the failings of matriarchs were tolerated. Georgina and Robert would grace the middle of the table, arbiters of sense and peace. Stephen had dubbed Amy Burton a clever woman, but believed that an intelligent woman could override the clever. But he had underestimated Amy. She was more than clever. She was bold, a rebel undisguised, as the clever rarely are. One looked for undercover maneuvers, missing the obvious. An intelligent woman was not likely to be influenced by such a one, but there were kernels of wisdom in her words and more importantly in her heart, and wisdom trumped intelligence. it was a force the intelligent had to reckon with, respect, and perhaps, just perhaps heed later, later! Now Julia would attend to more mundane matters. The bathroom plumbing was on today's agenda and then Stephen's guest list for the long-awaited happy event celebrating her brother Jonathan's return.

# CHAPTER THIRTEEN

Julia usually enjoyed the long walk to the Maltby mansion, but the excitement in preparing for her brother's arrival had tired her, so this day she opted for the carriage to take her there and return her home. She would then be fresh and alert for Stephen's recounting of the day's events. At first they had bored her, but she soon realized she was learning about finance and trade as few other women would. She followed up his recitals with information gleaned from the Langley library. Music, literature and art, which she most wished to read about, were available with her library subscription and from books borrowed from friends, most notably from Lord Tilton's vast library and the Maltby mansion library, which caretaker Elsie had given her use of. Knowledge was available, and it was precious. As her carriage drew near the mansion Julia saw the curtain part in the morning room and the familiar face watching her approach.

"Elsie! How does your garden grow?"

"Beautifully, come see," and the caretaker led her through the rooms stopping at the windows in each to talk about the flowers they bore. Since she could not attend to the lawn the family had engaged a man for monthly mowings. The gardens had moved indoors, where Elsie could manage them and the rooms came alive with color as the perimeters and tables bloomed.

"I see you've had your exercise Elsie. Your bright eyes and ruddy complexion tell me so."

"Indeed, after tending to my flowers with the windows wide open I have done my shaking exercises. I do not enjoy shaking the muslin covering all the seating in the mansion, but a little each day keeps me healthy and the seating clean. I need not inform you of the postboy's last news and gossip. It centered on your brother's expected arrival in London. You must be so happy."

"I am, Elsie, and privately I tell you I'm wondering if he will be the same Jonathan of his youth. Life experiences do affect a person."

"They do, but human nature resists change. What was he like in earlier days?"

"Exuberant, enthusiastic, eager for challenges and the opportunity to overcome them, a happy boy."

"I doubt such a one will be changed, but his application of those traits may. He has been exposed to different circumstances. And you, my dear, what adventures have befallen you since last we met?"

Julia hesitated.

"You may speak freely to your friend. The walls have ears, but there is no one they can tell."

"A handsome man has, for no reason at all, taken an interest in me."

Elsie chuckled. "Obviously there is nothing about you that would interest a man. Has he a particular purpose, do you think?"

"I fear it is not a moral one."

"You have decided not to give back Stephen some of his own, then? The postboy keeps me well-informed."

"Gracious, no! One fool in a marriage is enough."

"And would it be foolish to yield to the young man?"

"You're teasing me. Retribution is not part of my nature."

"It is not retribution if you care for him."

"He's pleasant enough, but I don't care in the way he might like. Why should I?"

"That question raises other questions. What are his attributes? How does he make you feel when you are with him? Why are you with him if you don't care for him?"

"It started on Mount Street" And she relayed their chats on the bench, at the subscription library, at the Langley Library where he taught her to play the mandolin, and to casual sightings and greetings as she moved about the city."

"What do you know about him?"

"Nothing, except that his behavior is pleasant, he has artistic interests and Lord Tilton thinks well of him and his work as temporary handyman."

Elsie looked intently at Julia, and the younger woman lowered her eyes.

"What are you doing about the problem with Stephen?"

"I must determine the extent of the problem. My aunt is working on it." She spoke into her lap.

"Lady Brighton — a formidable woman, and an exacting one. I have no doubt she will remove the merchandise as a start."

"Yes, I am blessed with her affection."

"You are indeed. Every family should have a Lady Brighton. Next, I assume, she will reduce the desire for the merchandise. Your head is well-advised to trust her. Your heart should consider additional arrangements."

"Such as?"

"The assistance of A London Lady."

"I would be too embarrassed to have a private matter paraded before the city."

"Embarrassment lasts a short while. Rectification of the problem lasts a lifetime."

"Her identity and whereabouts are unknown, and I think it for the best."

Elsie smiled. "One can do so much under cover of mystery. But if she is made aware of Stephens's wanderings, she may choose to assist you. Consider it. You deserve more than financial security. You haven't seen the flowers in the library, my new pansies."

Julia accompanied Elsie to the library where the flowers magnificently adorned a corner table. She stopped short in her admiration as her eyes alighted on some slim volumes behind the flowers.

"What is this? You read the infamous London Lady?"

"One must have some excitement to enliven the solemn quiet in this mansion. Do you not do the same during quiet times at home?"

Julia laughed. "I would deny it to Stephen, but I do. It's hard to resist hearing of scandals, as long as they are not your own."

"Yet I don't believe A London Lady designs her stories with scandal in mind. They may entertain the masses, but they perform a service in informing wives of their husband's indiscretions. How can women do something about the situation if they do not know it exists?"

"The author has a lucrative profession."

"You think she does this for the money? I rather think her income goes to the informants who provide her with so much text. My postboy informs me there are many servants who now dress above their station."

"Your postboy is better informed than mine, who is speaks little and knows even less."

"My solitary situation may encourage him to enliven my days with news. Fortunately I am solitary only six months a year, and I can spend the other six at home."

"You never speak of your home, only the home of your youth."

"At my time of life memories hold the heart in thrall and are relived in the sharing. You speak little of your married life. It is only through gossip, usually a distorted medium of information, that I hear of it."

"A rebuke well given, Elsie. Is there anything I can bring you on my next visit?"

"No, dear, your presence is all that I desire."

******

Julia returned home to find Lady Brighton in the morning room.

"Apple cider in the library," ordered Lady Brighton.

Julia nodded her agreement, and Maggie hurried off to fetch it.

"Success, my dear, success," was all her aunt said until both they and the libation were in the library and the door shut and locked.

"Besides the baker's wife there are two women he sees. One is the young wife of an old member of Parliament, the other the middle-aged wife of a shipbuilder."

"Are they in love with him?"

"Julia, even knowledgeable servants can't read minds, but it would seem they are using him as he is using them. Both husbands are very occupied with their work. The politician talks politics constantly and is off frequently to meetings on matters of public concern which are of no concern to his wife. The shipbuilder is more occupied with his vessels than with his wife's, and dresses as men did ten years ago. She constantly complains she is embarrassed to be seen with such a dowdy-looking man, but he insists that wealth enables him to dress as he pleases and still retain the respect due him."

"What about Stephen attracts them?"

"The young one, his attention and his gifts. She's been heard to say she's a married widow for all the time her husband spends with her or on her. But Stephen may have to downplay the gifts if she wishes to display them. Her husband has criticized what he believes are her expenditures on them."

"And I with trepidation have to ask for an increase in the household allowance!"

"The middle-aged woman is flattered that a younger, well-dressed man, a lord no less, finds her attractive."

"And what do you think was Stephen's motivation for choosing them?"

"They were accessible and undemanding. Why would a man with a beautiful, charming wife choose them or anyone? It's also probably the thing to do at his club. Several butlers have volunteered that these marital side dishes are a constant source of conversation at certain men's clubs. To be an insider you apparently need a woman on the side. I suggest you urge Stephen to join a less demanding club. He'll be forced to do so anyway when evidence of his being a blackguard is tossed in his face."

"He will deny as he has before all accusations of infidelity if I insist he change clubs."

"So don't suggest it. I will threaten the wives that their husbands will be informed of their liaisons. That should remove these two pieces of merchandise from the market. If it doesn't we inform the husbands."

"With words or with proof?"

"Proof would be better, but more costly. Words will probably achieve the same effect. Words first."

"I would like to meet these women."

"Oh Julia, that's a terrible idea. You know enough."

"I am curious. We are sharing the same man."

"I forbid it! I myself will approach the women. My authoritative presence may produce the desired result. It's been effective in the past. Then we remove Stephen's temptation to sin, beginning with his club membership. My nephew's secret behavior is a scourge on the family name. Since the family name cannot be removed the scourge must be. I will leave you now. You have much to do preparing for Jonathan's celebratory dinner. At least that's a happy event to look forward to. Be of good cheer, Julia, and leave this Stephen matter in my hands."

# CHAPTER FOURTEEN

Julia's lady's maid looked with satisfaction at her handiwork. Julia's hair, upswept and captured in a ribbon sparkling with faux pave diamonds was elegant. The dress that Julia had commissioned was pink, with cascading ruffles at neck and wrist. She would look a feminine and welcoming presence for Jonathan.

The carriage announced his arrival. He bounded up the steps and embraced his sister for so long that Stephen came to the door to see what was detaining him. All three spoke at once. expressing joy at seeing one another. Julia clasped his arm and exclaimed, "In all the years of my marriage I haven't seen you once. Were handwritten notes several times a year the best you could do?"

"Darling Julia, I would much rather have spent my time with you than fighting the infidels intent on tyrannizing the continent."

They embraced once more, then Jonathan was afforded a tour of the house and his quarters decorated in navy-blue and white and lumber brown, his favorite colors. They then repaired to the dining room for a hearty meal of turkey in gravy, sweet potatoes, lima beans and vintage wine. For dessert Julia herself had baked a cinnamon apple pie, which produced additional shows of affection from her happy brother.

"After shipboard rations, this dinner is ambrosial. When we weren't in hand-to-hand combat warding off the French attempting to board our vessel, we spent days on end preventing food supplies from reaching their men on shore rather than eating food ourselves."

"Could you not eat the provisions captured?"

"No, Stephen, those were to be remanded to the British government, and when they sold the goods, we got our share of the proceeds. More is yet to come, as the sales continue. Now that Napoleon has been trounced at Waterloo we have the leisure to collect and invest the bounty."

"I can help you with that, Jonathan. At Liberty Bank we pride ourselves in making lucrative investments for our clients. How much do you expect your gain will amount to?"

"That isn't clear yet, but it will be a tidy sum, so much in fact that I can use part of it to buy an estate of my own."

"Do you expect to retire soon?"

"Within a few years. I wish to enjoy the new position I have had the honor of receiving. But I will be able to visit English soil more often, so I can purchase and organize an estate to be ready for the day I leave Service."

"You can also enjoy the significant increase in salary your new title affords. I hope you plan to reside near us."

"I can invest with you wherever in the country I live, though my choice would be an estate near my parents."

"Which is not so very far off."

"You are indeed a banker, Stephen,"

It was obvious Stephen took this as a compliment, but Jonathan's expression indicated this was not the case. The day grew dark, and the servants lit the candles on all the tables as conversation continued. Each was eager to hear news about the others, and it was beyond the bedtime of all before it ceased and they repaired to their chambers.

In the morning, after a breakfast of toast and jam, Stephen left for his stroll to the bank and Jonathan left for a stroll through London to see what changes time had wrought since his last visit years earlier. Julia supervised the cooking and cleaning that would prepare the house to receive the guests Stephen had chosen as privileged to attend a dinner celebrating the return of a hero from the recently concluded war against Napoleon.

******

It was eight o'clock, and horses' hoofs announced the arrival of the carriages bringing the guests who would dine with and honor Admiral Jonathan Geffen. For the first time at a dinner party, Stephen stood back, and Julia and Jonathan stood at the door greeting the guests, whom Jameson escorted to the drawing room, where lively conversations ensued about the war, London and the world. Forty minutes later the party repaired to the dining room, where place cards indicated who was to sit where, in the usual way, the host and hostess at the head and foot of the table, for this occasion with the hostess at the head. Stephen had demurred at inviting Amy Burton, who arrived alone, but Julia had stood firm. Lady Brighton came alone, Stephen never questioned his aunt's solitary appearance, and Amy would make an even sixteen at the table, and with Jonathan and Lord Tilton, an equal number of men and women. Although Julia parted Lord Tilton and Amy, she gave her old friend the advantage of at least looking at his beloved across the table, though at opposite ends of their respective sides. Stephen frowned that Amy was seated close to them and almost directly across from Jonathan, but there was nothing he could do about it without creating a fuss.

The table groaned with the huge number of dishes heaped upon it through course after course. All the servants were on hand to expedite removal of the dishes and, at Julia's raised hand, to bring in the dishes that comprised succeeding courses.

During the first course Stephen made the rounds of the table, chatting briefly with the men and complimenting their wives. He repeated this during the second and third courses. Talk inhibited overeating, which was just as well, since some of Stephen's business clients had expansive middles barely contained by their pants. A choice of coffee or tea ended the meal, coffee especially preferred by the men who had imbibed copious amounts of wine. As the women's cups were smaller, they were spared ungraceful waddles as they rose from time to time.

Between chats with Georgina Julia scanned the table as she ate. She noted that Stephen did likewise, but that his gaze fell too often on two of the party, Mrs. Cartwright, wife of a member of Parliament and Mrs. Williams, wife of a coal merchant. At their chats before dinner Julia had heard of the tribulations suffered by the Parliamentarian's wife, as five children under the age of eight disregarded house rules, creating walking hazards in the parlor and nearly setting the house on fire as they lit and forgot unattended candles in their play skits. She longed for respite from the chaos, but her husband was building them a nest egg and had no time for games or discipline of the children. Would she be interested in interludes with Stephen as an escape, wondered Julia. And the coal merchant's wife said she had had enough of seeing coal under his fingernails and smelling coal on the person of her husband at dinnertime and in bed. Would she be interested in spending time with a man who smelled of French cologne and whose fingernails were cut and clean? Julia chastised herself for such thoughts. Why was she assuming these women would submit to the salacious suggestions of a married man? But Stephen's roving eyes convinced her that Stephen would try. For Stephen this was an evening for business, official and private. Julia looked at Lady Brighton. Engaged in conversation with Lord Tilton she was unaware of the additional burden she might have to assume after this evening. She might throw up her hands in despair and abandon the quest for justice for Julia and reform of her nephew.

But now from the corner of her eyes Julia noticed something else. Jonathan kept requesting food beyond his reach on the table. She had placed his favorites close at hand, yet he kept asking Robert across the table who was asking Amy who was closer to the dishes to pass the boiled turkey or boiled peas, both of which he detested, or the hare soup, when the transparent at his elbow was his favorite. Robert was vexed.

"Jonathan, my hand is tiring of transporting your meal across the table, would you like to change seats with me?"

Jonathan rose with alacrity and did just that.

Julia looked at Lord Tilton's face which bore an expression of panic, which was quickly justified. Suddenly Jonathan's interest in food disappeared. Julia could not hear what he was saying but the look on his face spoke volumes. At their assembly in the drawing room before dinner he had spent considerable time talking to Amy. She was an accomplished woman. While her late husband had attended to his trade she had become proficient in knowledge of Greek and Roman sculpture and was soon to give a talk on the subject at Wigley's Royal Promenade Rooms, which had an exhibition of such sculpture. She was also proficient in French. Was Jonathan sharing his exiting experiences in trouncing the French in the war just ended? It looked more like he was anticipating exciting experiences in the battle of the sexes. Lord Tilton suddenly rose, his face flushed, and offered a toast to the hero of the war. All guests followed him, raised their glasses in salute to Jonathan and downed the libation, after which they applauded the young man. Jonathan rose, bowed deeply and thanked them for the honor, saying that he was just one of many who deserved to be recognized for valor in the war. Hopefully peace would reign for the remainder of their lifetimes. When he sat down only one arm was placed on the table. The whereabouts of the other was signified by a shriek from Amy, as an arm encompassed her waist. She raised her hand to execute a slap just as Julia shouted "Jonathan!" and a second hand on the table joined the first. Amy was now giving Jonathan a tongue-lashing and Lady Brighton was now at his side to join in disapproval.

"Ladies!" exclaimed Jonathan, "I meant no offense. I am a mere man deprived of female companionship of any duration for years. I have not presumed to act so with any of the other lovely ladies at the table. He pointed at the pudgy, double-chinned, rail-thin wives.

"The temptation to do so was great, but I chose an unmarried woman, hoping she would honor me with her attention."

"I am unmarried," Lady Brighton stated stoutly.

"And I could never neglect your lovely presence as well, but in respect to my brother-in-law I did not think it seemly to make advances to his aunt."

"Or perhaps you feared her arm, strong as a boulder, would knock you flat if you did."

"That too, Lady Brighton. But I apologize for my unwelcome action. The wine has affected my behavior in ways unnatural to me." He turned to Amy. "Will you forgive me?"

"The Bible says you must," affirmed Robert from across the table.

Amy was silent.

"So it does," affirmed Lady Brighton, reluctantly. "Does it not also say something about not tampering with the assigned seating at dinner?" And she returned to her seat.

"No, it does not," mumbled Robert. And then louder, "I did make a mistake."

"A whopper" said Mr. Williams seated the other side of Amy.

Jonathan looked at Amy. "I accept your apology," she said primly.

Georgina patted Robert's hand in consolation, then turned to Julia and whispered, "What next?"

Stephen sat stiffly, not daring to say a word. As the table was cleared for tea, coffee and dessert, mumblings and muted giggles could be heard. Suddenly something clattered to the floor. Amy's dessert spoon had fallen and she bent low to retrieve it without success. Jonathan lowered himself to the floor, lifted the tablecloth and surveyed the scene.

"There it is, behind Mrs. Cartwright's mutton. Mrs. Cartwright, would you please move your leg?"

"Where shall I move it?" she replied.

"To your right, to join you other leg — of lamb," he whispered.

Amy, watching the scene below the tablecloth, lifted her head and laughed.

Jonathan, still seated on the floor, beckoned her to lower her head to him, which she did.

"Please forgive me, Amy. I promise not to lose my head again, though I cannot guarantee not to lose my heart. You are too good, too fine for schoolboy behavior. Please accept my apology and your spoon."

Amy laughed heartily. "I accept!"

Jonathan rose to his seat. All eyes were upon them.

"She dropped a spoon," he explained.

Titters turned to guffaws and outright laughter.

"Any interesting activity going on under the table?" queried Mrs. Cartwright.

"No," replied Jonathan. "All shoes are properly shod and ready to be seen as means of transport. While floored I also took the opportunity to apologize once more for the knavishly nautical behavior to which you were recently a witness."

Mrs. Cartwright turned to her husband. "During our next dispute dear, do take to the floor. Your view of things may be more enlightened and I may be more persuaded to appreciate your political views."

Jonathan and Amy's faces were now blazing red, and the table was in convivial uproar. Lord Tilton's face was likewise red, with fury. After beverages were drunk and pastry devoured the women retired to the drawing room, leaving the men to the usual stag end-of-evening talk and drinking more wine than was good for them. Lady Brighton begged an early leave, an uncontrollable scowl and slight limp indicating the reason.

As the women dropped into chairs and onto the sofa in the drawing room Mrs. Cartwright turned a gleeful face to her companions. "I haven't had such an exciting evening in years! Oh, Amy, to be boldly approached by a young, handsome man, a war hero no less —I would have been so flattered!"

"I would have been outraged — to think I would abandon my marriage vows to indulge in whatever obscene, unholy activities he was requesting." Mrs. Williams shuddered.

"I didn't say I would submit, Dahlia, but it would be refreshing to hear I still retained enough beauty and charm to interest a young man."

"From where I sat it didn't look like Jonathan was propositioning Amy. He wasn't asking, he was taking."

"Oh, Amy, do tell us what he said and how you felt!"

Amy looked at the eager faces around her. She barely knew these women. "I was both flattered and angry."

"A proper feeling," agreed Mrs. Williams, "but in what proportion. Oh — "Admiral Jonathan Geffen had just entered the drawing room.

"Pardon me, ladies, but the evening wears on, and our chance for conversation will soon be past." He turned to Amy. "I hear that the talk you will give on female dress in Greece at Wigley's Royal Promenade Rooms will be tomorrow. I would not miss it for the world. Would you kindly give me a private tour of the accompanying sculpture exhibit after your talk. I hear the exhibit overflows with visitors during regular viewing hours and I will only be in London three days more. Would it be too much to ask you to accord me this privilege?"

"I'll be tired after speaking for an hour. I will ask one of the knowledgeable docents to accompany you and explain the exhibit."

"Your knowledge certainly surpasses the docents' or they would be giving the talk. I hope my earlier foolish behavior is not the reason for your refusal to honor me with your guidance."

The wives gawked and looked in awe at Amy.

"I —I don't think it would be proper for just the two of us to view the exhibit at that hour."

"I can accompany you, Amy." Lord Tilton had just entered the room. "You needn't be alone with one man late at night in a near-empty museum should you wish to acquiesce to the Admiral's request."

"Being alone with two suitors is much the better," agreed Mrs. Cartwright, with a twinkle in her eyes.

Jonathan and Lord Tilton blushed profusely.

"Will you, please," pleaded Jonathan. "If you refuse I will believe it is because of my previous juvenile behavior for which I've apologized multiple times and which apology you have accepted."

"All right," agreed Amy reluctantly.

"Bravo!" exclaimed Mrs. Cartwright. "You'll be honoring the Greek heroes of past wars with a hero of the present. Will you allow Lord Tilton to act as chaperone? It would be proper to have one."

"It would be more appropriate to have another woman act in that capacity," said Mrs. Williams.

'I'm sure my husband would allow me that role," responded Mrs. Cartwright. "The children will be in bed and our evenings are so dull."

"No need to wrest you from your cozy home," said Julia, who had been silent all the while. "I shall be at Amy's talk, and I shall accompany her and Jonathan on the tour."

"But what about me? My offer still stands," said Lord Tilton. "Amy, would you mind very much if I were present on the tour?"

With a barely suppressed smile Amy replied, "Not very much."

So it was settled. Jonathan and Lord Tilton rejoined the men in the dining room, where talk, loud and boisterous could now be heard in the slurred attempts of the sloshed and slightly senseless.

"A little advice, Amy, on how to deal with this situation from my vast experience in these matters," said Mrs. Cartwright.

"Vast?" said Mrs. Williams. "You can't be much older than Amy."

"From earlier, youthful days, and from books. I read a lot."

"Perhaps you could write one," responded Mrs. Williams in a huff.

Mrs. Cartwright laughed, not in the least embarrassed.

At dinner Stephen Langley's eyes had often rested on Mrs. Cartwright. Julia mused that Stephen did not select victims. He chose like minds. He had also eyed Mrs. Williams, but a moralist was obviously beyond his reach. "I have a lifetime of this ahead of me," thought Julia. "I need advice from someone totally uninvolved with my problem. God bless Lady Brighton and her efforts on my behalf, but I must speak to Elsie at the Maltby mansion. Perhaps her caring, wise advice will produce a spark of light that can grow into a solution. I am so unhappy!" Her eyes turned to her companions. They were bombarding a silent Amy with advice.

******

Stephen had gone to bed, leaving Julia to upbraid her brother.

"How could you, Jonathan. And in front of all our guests!"

"I can't waste time, Julia. In three days I leave my darling sister to visit our parents. Amy is besieged by suitors. I want to remain in her memory as one of them before I am able to return. I'll be making day trips from our childhood home to examine properties between there and London. I aim to purchase 2,000 acres of prime farmland, build a palatial mansion to occupy in a few years when I retire from the Royal Navy, and have an estate my wife and I can be proud of. Additional acreage will follow."

"Can you manage the expense?"

"Oh, yes. We've captured so many enemy ships, all loaded with provisions, that the government stipend for this bounty has increased my wealth beyond my dreams. I'm thirty-five, and not likely to amass much more wealth even as an admiral. I'll become a gentleman farmer like father, only bigger and faster."

"If you want a family, realize that Amy is over forty. She and her husband were married for over ten years before he passed and they had no children."

"The fault may have been his, but it matters not. I would rather play ball with a son and dance with a sweet little girl than change linens and attend to the midnight howls of infants. Children born at the age of five or six would be ideal and less stress on my wife. In institutions and on the streets of London there are so many homeless children, without parents, without the bare necessities of life, without love. I would be happy to adopt at least two and give them a present and a future to enjoy."

"You've met women on shore leave, have you not. Did none of them strike your fancy?"

"I've met plenty! Most were giddy young things without significant thoughts in their heads, fine for an evening of fun, but not for a lifetime. And none of the others stopped my heart the way Amy Burton does. if I delay another man is likely to carry her off. What a woman — bold, brave, brainy, with a taste for adventure, ripe and rare!"

"But has she shown any interest in you?"

"She is a woman who will think about what she has seen of me, and compare me to her other suitors. If Lord Tilton is representative of the lot I'll look more exciting."

"One is a member of Parliament and the other a wealthy merchant."

"Dull professions and possibly boring men. I'm hoping an exciting woman would not be attracted to a mundane life. We would live in the romantic countryside and spend the Season enjoying the culture of London. What woman would not enjoy that? You will help me, won't you Julia? I know Lord Tilton is a friend, but I am your brother. Mention me often to her, in favorable terms of course, Meanwhile I shall forward my case after the lecture at the private tour that will be as private as a walk through Hyde Park, but - oh well. In addition, I shall learn something. The influence of ancient Greek fashion on women's clothes today is important information for all men."

Julia laughed, Jonathan winked, and they parted for their respective bedchambers.

# CHAPTER FIFTEEN

"The lecture room at Wigley's was packed with women. The only men present were Admiral Jonathan Geffen, Gerald, Lord Tilton and Edward Riley. Apparently women speakers on female garb of antiquity did not attract men. The room was large. Posters, drawings and paintings on easels left and right depicted women in Hellenistic garb. GREEK INFLUENCE ON MODERN FEMALE DRESS also drew several of London's best seamstresses. After a sip of water from a glass on a table on the platform Amy began her talk. Garment flow was detailed, reasons for the thinness of the outer garments and the existence of multiple undergarments were explained, as were necklines that dived between the breasts. Not neglected were sleeves, short and long, and gloves. Where had modern dress modified the Greek heritage and why? Heads turned left and right as Amy spoke and moved among the illustrations. Overhead chandeliers filled the room with light. The applause at the conclusion of the talk seemed bound to continue indefinitely, stopped only by Amy's departure from the platform. The women's eyes shone with delight, the men's with amazement at what they had heard and seen. As the audience rose to depart so did the gas-lit chandeliers, plunging the room into total darkness. A member of the institution called for calm, bellowing that the staff had candles and would lead them to the exit. Lord Tilton and Edward Riley sprang into action, helping to lead the women from the lecture room. Jonathan was not among them. He had inquired about the speaker's exit path and was at her side in the back of the room when the lights gave up the ghost. He pinned her against the wall, he told her, to allow the agitated females to exit, because "as the captain is the last to leave the ship, so must a speaker be the last to leave the lecture room."

"You were wonderful, you are wonderful, such knowledge, such poise. It was a pleasure to listen to your presentation." He lifted a candle which conveniently appeared at his side and looked her full in the face. "You're very beautiful, you know. Women may have to modify their dress, as you said, to suit their needs, but you would look ravishing in anything you chose to wear."

Amy attempted to move, but the wall was at her back and both Jonathan's hands were upon it, which prevented her moving left or right. The term "ravishing" disturbed her.

"Thank you, Jonathan, but I would like to join the audience exiting, and as a gentleman I hope you will allow me to do so."

Jonathan moved back a bit and removed his hands from the wall.

"The light outage prevents you from honoring me with a tour of the exhibit. I'll be leaving in a few days, and I'd like to take this opportunity to talk to you. I doubt if you'll allow me any other time, and I've something serious to say."

A small smile appeared on Amy's face. "You must be desperate to talk if you consider this blackout an opportunity."

An exiting woman gave a shriek as she slammed into a barrier.

"I am. I've never met a woman like you. During the visit to my parents I will be examining properties nearby, between the old homestead and London, with the intention of buying at least 2,000 acres of land and designing a mansion to go with it. If you marry me the design will be yours. We'll be landowning gentry and able to travel to Paris, Rome, wherever you like, Greece, if it suits you. I don't need your money, don't want it. We'll have a marriage contract leaving it solely in your possession."

Amy Burton was dumbfounded. She breathed out deeply. "But I barely know you, and your knowledge of me is no better!"

"I'm sure of my heart. You're a good woman, an intelligent woman, a delicious woman, and I want you to be my wife. I know you're not one to act in haste, but tell me you'll consider my proposal."

"You will surely want children."

"I want whatever you want, any way you want it. I'll see you one more time before I leave, at the ball Lord Tilton is giving to celebrate our victory over Napoleon. If you can give me an answer then, I leave for the countryside with joy. If you require more time I'll understand and hope that upon my return in a few weeks you will allow me to call on you, make you better acquainted with me and press my suit once more."

The room was no longer plunged in darkness. Attendants had reignited the lights on each chandelier and Amy and Jonathan turned to face one of them and the members of the audience at his side —Julia, Lady Brighton and a flushed Lord Tilton.

"So gad you're all right, Mrs. Burton. We'll keep the lights on until you are ready to leave."

Jonathan turned to Lord Tilton. "You needn't take me back with Julia, Gerald, I have a carriage waiting," he said smoothly, and he departed. Attendants awaited him in the lobby, and he gave each a goodly sum. "In appreciation for the darkness," he said.

In the lecture room Lord Tilton faced Amy. "What did he say!" he demanded. "Omit nothing, what did he tell you?"

"He said I am ravishing. He complimented my character, my intelligence, my movements. And he said I was delicious."

"He dared to address you that way? The impudent scoundrel! I hope you boxed his ears most soundly!"

"Why? Do you not agree with his sentiments?"

"Of course I agree, but I would never phrase them in such an offensive manner!"

"I was surprised, shocked and embarrassed by his words, but I was not offended. Beyond your gifts and genteel words how have you expressed an interest in me?"

"In a more honorable way. All the world knows you do not address a lady as he did."

"He was not addressing the world, he was addressing me. Are you saying no words of passion would ever escape your lips, that no smouldering desire would appear in your face, that no action would proceed from that desire, no indication be shown a lady of an inkling of what resides in your heart?"

"I've given more than an inkling," he responded stoutly.

"Well it's not enough!" And she turned her back to him and left the room.

Lord Tilton turned a forlorn look at lady Brighton. "Margaret, what shall I do?"

"She told you, Gerald."

******

Lord Tilton's carriage was at the curb. He helped Julia into it. and climbed in beside her, leaning back heavily in the seat.

"She wants to be romanced, but that's not my way. Show me how, Julia. I'd be ever so grateful."

"Think of all the socially unacceptable words you would like to say to her and all the actions you would like to take and say them and do them."

"My God, she'll think I want to bed and board her!"

"Don't you?"

"I want more than that."

"I know you do Gerald, but you'll never get to that if she doesn't see the besotted lover. She'll stop you if you go too far."

"Are there any classes in this?" he asked hopefully.

"One, and it's free. It's in your heart. Go there, listen, learn, and let it out, do not hold back. At least not in front of Amy."

"Do you really think she would be interested?" he asked despondently.

"She's all but hit you over the head with what she wants. Of course she's interested!" The horses came to a stop in front of the Langley home, and Lord Tilton helped her from the carriage.

"Behaving in such a way is new to me."

"At times we must all behave in new ways. Trust in yourself." She kissed his cheek and entered the house, dismayed. Her friend had the desire, but not the faith.

******

Julia was surprised at the arrival of Lady Brighton before noon the next day.

"Forgive me, dear. I know I will see you at Lord Tilton's ball tonight, but I was eager to share with you the results of my marital interference. I discovered a third woman who has been cavorting with Stephen even longer than the initial two we were aware of. I contacted them all.

This is the note each received:

> IF YOU DO NOT END YOUR LIAISON WITH LORD LANGLEY YOUR HUSBAND WILL BE INFORMED.
>
> INDICATE YOUR RESPONSE, RESEAL THIS NOTE AND RETURN IT TO THE MESSENGER.

I left it unsigned. The wife of the member of Parliament, no, not Mrs. Cartwright, responded, 'The liaison is over.' The shipbuilder's wife reluctantly agreed. But the newly discovered infidel, the wife of a coal merchant, responded, 'There is no liaison.' The wife of the member of Parliament kept her word. Her scheduled meeting with Stephen the following night was not held, as my informant told me. No further assignations have been arranged between Stephen and the shipbuilder's wife. I sent another note to the coal merchant's wife. Here it is:

> THIS IS YOUR FINAL WARNING. END YOUR LIAISON WITH STEPHEN LANGLEY.
> YOUR RESPONSE:

Her response was 'Find me a married substitute and I will drop Lord Langley.'

"I'm asked to be a party to her infidelity with someone else!"

"Is this the pious Mrs. Williams who was at our recent dinner party?"

"It is. An excellent actress is she not?"

"And she wants another married man?"

"Yes, it's protection. If the woman wants to break from the affair and the man refuses she can threaten to tell his wife. If he has no wife, he can threaten to tell her husband. She has no leverage."

"You can't find her someone else's husband!"

"Of course not. At least Stephen's women are reduced by two. I could do as I said and send her husband a note revealing the affair, but she would deny it, and my accusation is unsigned. Worse yet, a check on her reputation revealed she is considered to be a model wife and a vocal member of the Women's League Against Prostitution, which she joined two years ago, probably when she began her affair with Stephen. She's covered her tracks well. No one is likely to believe an accusation of infidelity against her. More likely they will believe someone jealous of her piety is trying to destroy her reputation. If other women join Stephen's pipeline we can reduce if not eliminate their number with notes similar to the ones I sent. I know this is not what you want to hear, but there it is."

"I can't saddle you with this hopeless quest for morality in Stephen, Aunt Margaret. You're entitled to enjoy your life."

"Nonsense, we've only just begun. It is time to inaugurate the second part of our plan, to make Stephen jealous of another man's interest in you. Wherever you go men look at you with admiration, but are too decent to do more. You need someone willing to at least appear to want to do more. Stephen stopped your mandolin lessons because he assumed your instructor had a personal interest in you. Edward Riley will attend Lord Tilton's gala tonight celebrating the end of our war with France. He will not be present in a menial capacity. I asked it of Lord Tilton as a favor, one of many I am able to call in. Talk with him, smile at him, laugh with him — in Stephen's presence. We shall see how much further we have to go with this charade to renew Stephen's exclusive interest in his wife."

"We can't use Edward Riley in this way. It isn't fair."

"You like each other's company. Nobody is being used. The situation is a natural convenience."

"And is this to go on for another fifty or sixty years?"

"No, dear. Long before that you will tire of upsetting yourself over Stephen's shenanigans, you will have children to love and occupy your time and you will continue to be a role model for our sex. You can't control Stephen's life, but you can control your own. You will find something enjoyable in each day. Little joys mount. A man should not be the be-all and end-all of happiness. Today, for example, you have a wonderful celebration to look forward to, so look forward, prepare, enjoy!"

# CHAPTER SIXTEEN

No one who was anyone wanted to miss Lord Tilton's gala celebration of the end of the war, but not everyone could be invited. Three hundred in the mansion's ballroom was the most his lordship could comfortably accommodate. Jonathan, handsome in his blue and white uniform, looked elegant, and Stephen in red and white silks looked like the first-born of his father, not the second. After much indecision, Julia had chosen the dress in pale blue organza, with barely any sleeves, a neckline plunging to the high waist and a mostly bare back. It was the most daring of her dresses, and she could foresee little use for it, but it was beautiful. Its appearance in a French magazine had so entranced her that she had bought the fabric from Robert and promptly had her dressmaker produce the garment before she could change her mind. Lord Tilton's gala would be an exceptional event. That was her excuse for choosing this dress this evening. It was a perfect choice for seducing a man, but that was hardly her interest. Stephen had not seen it before, and his eyes blazed approval when he did. The barouche was the vehicle of choice for the fifteen-minute ride to the Tilton estate and Reggie had brought it 'round to the front of the residence. The open-air gig would have bowed to the elements, and the elements were blowing hard. It was growing dark, and the sights of London were barely visible through the fog, but the air was crisp and refreshing and the trio enjoyed the ride to the Tilton mansion just outside London.

Every window of the mansion was alight with candles waving a greeting to incoming guests who mounted the broad steps to the entrance where a concierge took their wraps, and gave them numbered tickets before the majordomo waved them toward the ballroom, where Lord Tilton stood, tall and regal, greeting the incoming guests. The double doors were open to reveal a ballroom glittering with thousands of lights on the cut-glass chandeliers and the sound of Handel's Water Music thundering a jubilant welcome. The room was awash with pastels, and Julia was glad she had chosen the powder blue gown. It was not for her to stand out this day, or any day, really. There were women present who dressed with more daring, but she reflected that fabrics and décolletage that revealed too much of what the dress contained were inappropriate for this occasion, or any other, except attendance at a house of ill repute. She blushed sightly at this thought, and pulled the sides of her diving neckline a bit closer together. She scanned the room for those she knew. Aunt Margaret had arrived and Georgina and Robert as well, but Edward Riley was not there. Across the room near the refreshments Amy Burton was chatting with the member of Parliament who was currently courting her. Had she come with him? Lord Tilton had greeted the last of his guests and was chatting with Lord Willie. Jonathan had left Julia's side upon entering the ballroom and was now making a beeline to Amy and the politician. Suddenly Julia saw Edward. He approached Lord Tilton, spoke briefly to him and took a path that led him past Julia.

"Good evening, Lady Langley." He bowed and moved on. What more could she expect?

Lord Tilton, recognizing that the music master was capable of following the planned program of music and entertainment, left Lord Wilie's side to concentrate on what he could not control — the movements of Amy Burton. But his movement toward her was at a snail's pace, as guests waylaid him to talk of this and that, and before he was able to reach her the music master announced the first of the evening's entertainment. An acrobatic act would recall the bravery of the British on land and sea. Dressed in army and navy garb they proceeded to do battle with the French army and navy. Landscapes and three-dimensional ships were wheeled in from the sides and were engaged in the plot. The guests roared with approval as the French army and fleet were defeated. Julia scoured the room for Jonathan. He had not left the side of Amy Burton. As she proceeded to move on to chat with other guests, he moved with her and joined the conversation. They danced several dances, which Lord Tilton's face indicated was unpardonable. Lord Tilton now approached Julia who was chatting with Georgina.

"Excuse me, ladies. I am appalled but don't know what to do. When I approached Amy to ask her to dance, Jonathan spoke before she could respond and said that she had promised the next dance to him. From the expression on her face I could see that she had promised no such thing."

"He is an admiral and a war hero," said Georgina. "This celebration is about him. If he asks Amy to dance and she refuses, society decrees that she can dance with no one else this evening."

"Amy does not always follow society's rules," countered Lord Tilton. "She is an independent woman."

"Tonight, apparently, she is going by them."

He turned to Julia. "Please ask your brother to dance so I can have some time on the dance floor with Amy."

"I will," and Julia made her way to Jonathan, arriving at the dance's end. She tapped him on the shoulder and extended her arms. The member of Parliament was on his way to Amy, but Lord Tilton's long legs brought him there first. At his approach Julia stepped aside, and with a signal to the music master with one hand and his arm around Amy's waist with the other Lord Tilton began to dance a waltz. Murmurs of delight wafted around them and other couples began to dance.

The politician shook his head. "If we have more such dance influences from the Continent we will have no morals left in England."

"Country dances will follow soon, I'm sure," consoled Georgina, as she and Robert danced by.

But before they did, the next entertainment took place. A trio of singers gave tribute to the British military with a heartfelt rendition of "The Soldier in a Foreign Land," followed by a salute to the British flag which descended from the ceiling and hovered over the guests. The military men in attendance were asked to raise their hands, and a long, warm ovation was accorded them. And now a young man with a mandolin took center stage. Edward Riley played and sang Beethoven's "Parting."

> Here is the fateful moment!
> farewell, my Berenice!
> My beloved, how shall I live
> so far away from you?
> I shall always live in sorrow,
> I shall have peace no longer;
> and you — who knows
> if you will ever remember me!

The applause for his performance lasted several minutes, prolonged by many women with tearstained faces. Edward bowed and left the platform. He moved toward Julia. Her heart beat faster and she clutched Georgina's hand. He spoke not a word, merely bowed to her and her friends, and moved on. Stephen continued his conversation with Lord Willie and Georgina pulled Julia away into a corner.

"Julia, get hold of yourself! He is gone for the evening and will soon be gone from London. The danger is past." But with one look at her friend's face she saw her error.

The ballroom was a swirl of movement and color, with the musicians drowning out the voices of the celebrants. Waiters moved fluidly but carefully around dancers and clusters of immobile guests. Stephen glanced at his watch and turned to his wife.

"Julia, it's almost time for Lord Tilton to mount the platform and announce the Deluge, to release the balloons on the ceiling and usher in the final dances and the extinguishing, one by one, of the lights in the chandelier. Where is he? Find him quickly, dear, before drinks and dancing fell his guests and the balloons descend without him."

A survey of the ballroom made it clear Lord Tilton was not there. Julia made her way to the exit with as much speed as spectators rooted in their places would allow. A servant carrying away an empty tray of sweets might know.

"He entered the library ten minutes ago, m'lady. He may still be there."

She hurried to his lordship's spacious library, from which she had borrowed many books in the past, and entered the room. Lord Tilton and Amy Burton were engaged in a heated dispute.

"You allow him to put his arm around your waist and let it remain?"

"I allowed no such thing. I attempted to move away, but his grip was firm, like his arguments in Parliament. Would you rather I had slapped his face and made a spectacle a dozen people would witness and spread throughout London?"

"To his disgrace."

"And to your dishonor. You know he's been my escort to many events in the past, yet you invited him. Did you think he would turn gentleman because he was your guest?"

"You could have dug your heels into his feet. He would have howled and released you with no one the wiser as to the source of the pain. A discarded suitor should know when he has lost the prize."

"A prize, am I, to be won? No one wins Amy Burton. She belongs to no one but herself. And what of your behavior? Watching and doing nothing! If you wanted a scene created, why did you not create it? Did you pull him away from me, did you land a powerful punch to his chin, as it is reputed you were wont to do in your youth?

## SONDRA LUGER

Did you clasp me to your bosom and shower kisses upon my face and neck? How dare you criticize my behavior when you —"

But she was unable to finish, for Lord Tilton had clasped her to his bosom and was doing as she had directed and his heart desired.

'Like this?" he murmured.

"Exactly like this," she whispered.

A long kiss ensued, Julia did not know how long, for she quietly opened the door and left the room. Hurrying toward her down the corridor was Edward Riley.

"Lady Langley! I was hoping to see you alone. "You look so well." His eyes gorged on her beautiful self. "Are you enjoying the festivities?"

Julia's eyes filled with anger, and fury convulsed her very being. Polite, formal, mundane. How she hated him! She sharply turned her back and hurried to the mansion's entrance just as a beaming Lord Tilton and a smiling Amy Burton exited the library. Lord Tilton grasped Edward's hands.

"You see before you the happiest man in the world!"

"If you wish your guests to be aware of your happiness, then by all means do not remove the lip rouge that marks your entire face."

"Oh my!" exclaimed Amy, removing a handkerchief from her reticule and removing the traces of his happiness.

"You may leave them, my darling."

"I may be brazen, my dear, but not bold enough to announce our happiness in such a blatant way to hundreds of strangers."

"We may wait a bit to tell the world, but I must tell Julia. She will be so happy for us!"

"She is gone, just now, and in a great huff."

"What did you say to her?" demanded Amy.

"Nothing much. I greeted her, said she looked well —"

Amy and Lord Tilton looked at each other and shook their heads.

Lord Tilton was adamant. "Go after her, man! Don't stand there like a fool!"

At this moment Lord Langley approached. "Ah, I've found you Lord Tilton. The balloons are anxious to descend. Have you seen my wife?"

# CHAPTER SEVENTEEN

Elsie pressed more tea upon Julia as the agitated young woman recounted events of the night before.

"I felt warm and feverish. I rushed outside. I needed air! My heart was beating fast, my head was throbbing. I sat on a bench outside and leaned against the colonnade. The cool night air refreshed me, revived me, and I was soon able to rejoin the others."

"You are in love with him."

"I can't be, I mustn't be!"

"Nevertheless, you are." The old woman leaned back on the sofa, but the wrinkled face held fast to Julia's eyes. "Admit it, Julia, if not to others at least to yourself. If you hide the truth that resides in your heart, it will eventually turn against you. It will fester, invade your organs and corrupt your blood. Not only will you lose the one you love, you will lose your health. The man you love faces the same fate."

"But how can it be avoided when the situation is impossible to rectify? My life with Stephen can be improved, but Edward can have no place in it. Stephen will never give me a divorce. With Edward what can I be — a prostitute, a common-law wife?"

"Ah, yes, the philandering husband blocks the way to happiness. But you have forgotten your Sunday school lessons, dear. 'With God all things are possible.' And sometimes he uses the oddest people to achieve success. I will show you one. Come with me."

Elsie led Julia out of the drawing room, to the Great Hall, down the painting festooned corridor to the stairway that, left and right, spanned the entrance hall. Up they went, past shuttered rooms, to the vast master bedchamber of the Maltby mansion. The old woman seated herself at a pink-skirted dressing table. She opened a large jar and proceeded to apply volumes of white cream to her face. She extracted a clean white cloth from the drawer and wiped her face clean of the cream, the makeup, and the wrinkles. She removed the combs from her hair, and a cascade of long silky waves descended to her waist. The face she turned to Julia was that of a beautiful woman in her forties. It resembled the portrait in the front hall that greeted all guests, the portrait of Lady Maltby.

Julia bowed low and deeply, but her friend extended her hands and lifted her up.

"There's no need for that," she said, "or this," and she dabbled a clean white cloth on Julia's tear-stained face. "Come with me, dear. Over another cup of tea I will tell you my story and propose a happy ending to yours."

And she led the way back, down the massive staircase, past the dining room to the kitchen, where Julia watched as she prepared another kettle of water for tea. She handed Julia a tray, added two cups and the kettle and led the way back to the drawing room for their chat.

"When Lord Maltby died I had a decision to make, the biggest decision of my life. No, Julia, marrying him was not my biggest decision, it was an obvious one. Of course I would marry one of the wealthiest titled men in England. That was a given. I would have been a fool not to. No, dear, my biggest decision was arriving at a purpose in life. I had lived in my husband's shadow for twenty-five years. He had been my marionette. I had pulled the strings of his life and made him appear to be a man of strength and wisdom, someone to be reckoned with, admired. His mind was not especially acute. A wife can't expect everything. But there, you see, is where I found my purpose. And then he was gone. What contribution could I make now, and to whom? My contribution had been through my husband. Not only had I lost his companionship, I had lost my purpose.

"People have always interested me. In those twenty-five years I had met people of high estate, low estate and no estate, and I had discovered that some, especially those of high estate, behaved beneath their rank. I was especially appalled by their moral misbehavior. Women may foolishly bow to the will of rich and powerful men, or be coerced into doing so, and the wives of these immoral men are none the wiser. They work to justify their positions, to make their husbands proud of them, ignorant of the fact that their husbands are disgracing them. I decided on a mission to help our sex, to release those in bondage to immoral men, by exposing their wanton, disgusting behavior, and suggesting remedies.

"I was a prolific letter writer. Lord Maltby's correspondence was left for me to write and him to sign. I decided to continue writing. But now I would write stories to expose wayward husbands, to inform mistreated wives and to allow their anger and public rebuke to work for changes in the men and to improved marriages. The women themselves would have to act, not necessarily as my stories suggested, but act, and now they would have the knowledge that would lead them to do so. I made sure the names, the facts, the relationships would be obvious. Enter A London Lady. I had the determination and the wealth to achieve my purpose. I harnessed the knowledge of servants, who were happy to supplement their income with my generous stipends. For seven years I've enjoyed seeing the discomfort of men and the realignment of their marriages."

"You never exposed Stephen in your novellas."

"He began his unseemly activities three years ago, a year after you began your kind visits to me. I liked you and was reluctant to confront you with the truth. You are a sensitive young woman, inexperienced in dealing with such matters. You would be publicly embarrassed, and I wanted to spare you that. I hoped there could be another way to put things right. Now that you are aware of the truth, there is no need to fictionalize it. I want to help you find happiness before I leave."

"You're going away? But why?"

"I've fallen in love with my French publisher. Can you believe it? I didn't expect to fall in love, didn't know what love was, until my heart and mind were suffused with this man, this wonderful man who is intelligent, kind, and a godsend to the human race. Oh how wonderfully he treats people, and how his publications inform and uplift readers!"

"So he fell in love with the amazing Lady Maltby."

"No, he thought he was in love with Jenny Denby, wife of a wealthy tradesman, who hated Paris, an enlightened man, who trusted his wife to visit, unescorted, for long periods, a city where depravity is no sin! My darling believed this nonsense, a minor flaw that worked to my advantage. I will be contributing serious articles on the foibles of society to one of his publications. My purpose will be to enlighten, to get people thinking about things they take for granted. Making a dent in misaligned psyches is possible. I will be writing under the nom de plum of A Paris Lady, which is what I shall be. It has been my home for half of every year since my husband died."

"London will be the worse for your departure."

"I think not. Everywhere the story of A London Lady is told the fear of God will inspire men, and some women too, to tread the moral path and be a credit to themselves their families and their Maker. And they may well fear that A London Lady may return, and wonder at the coincidence of A Paris Lady not so far away."

"I shall miss my friend Elsie, the housekeeper."

# SONDRA LUGER

"She is gone forever, and she says good riddance to shaking dust covers off chairs and sofas daily. But I expect you and Eugenia will continue a friendship that began oddly. First, your story must have a happy ending. Love must triumph. Since you do not love your husband it must triumph with someone else."

"It's hard to imagine doing more than Lady Brighton has envisioned. Contentment, at the most, seems more likely than happiness, which seems impossible."

"You view it as impossible, so for you it is. If you consulted your friends, family, the rules of society they too would tell you it's impossible. They have no imagination. They see through a glass darkly. But A London Lady has changed lives by presenting other possibilities. You see before you the late Lady Maltby, but when I look in my glass I see A London Lady, a more significant and powerful person than the consort, the appendage, if you will, of the late Lord Maltby." She pointed to a table holding a dozen slim volumes of her writings. "For the past seven years I have guided philandering husbands and foolish wives. Recall the case of Mrs. Twitmire, pinning away because her husband sought younger, fresher fields several nights a week. She did her research in the lending library, saved most of her household allowance, managing the household on a frugal budget, and to the amazement of her husband left this paragon of virtue to reside in Bath and open a boarding house for visitors who came to take the waters. The accommodations were designed for the elite, the furniture, tapestries, fixtures familiar only to aristocrats, and indeed many stayed there. Her husband sought to confiscate her income, but since she saved it under another name, he could never discover where her growing wealth resided. In addition to enjoying the mineral baths, she was also enjoying the company of many titled men, but always, to their dismay, refusing to succumb to their physical desires. Her husband returned to her, his immorality dispatched, and on occasion it was he who required assistance from her financial largesse, the location of which remained a mystery forever. The London wife, in another story, did something similar, but in place of a boarding house she chose to create a bottled water establishment, which brought her into contact with a wealthy Scotsman and a new life in his homeland, her husband be damned. The real husband has still not lived down the disgrace of being abandoned by his wife, who is now living in a lifestyle he could never afford. And surely you remember the case of Mrs. McIvey, whose husband forced her to make do with a minimal budget so he could spend lavishly on his mistress. He was a bore, with no interest save his business and his nighttime paramour. The wife was no paragon of virtue either, but her irritability was largely due to an illness and its attending pain which no practitioner of the medical arts could relieve. Her butler, pitying her greatly, followed her to Brighton, where with the ability to extract sympathy, she extracted it from a banker, who lent her the money to start a school for butlers. It amazes me that in real life no one has thought to do so. Anyway, I'm sure you remember that her business flourished and she could afford to comb the country for those practiced in the art of medical and folk medicine. Her ailment disappeared, as did the crankiness it had produced. Lauded socially by residents and visitors to the town, her husband, hearing of this, appeared to relieve her of her wealth and discover what the hoopla was all about. He sought a reconciliation.  But an Austrian duke, on vacation there and interested in acquiring a butler, had become enamored of her, and she accepted his proposal of marriage. He spent a tidy sum verifying the well-known facts concerning the philandering husband and spent additionally to appeal to Parliament and the Church of England for a divorce. She moved to Austria, visiting her children in England several times a year.  Of course in real life the wife chose another route. She opened an imported jewelry establishment and when her reformed and remorseful husband begged her to return, she did. He was a bit of a bore, but she considered his boredom a small price to pay for the attention and gifts he was showering on her and for the right to raise her children. He was now running the jewelry establishment, the role of businesswoman did not interest her, and he was eager to take her to social events that mitigated the effect of his boredom. He was grateful to have her raise the children, who were affecting his mental health.

"So you see, dear Julia, that the solutions to the problems facing our heroines are merely suggestions which expand the thinking of the ladies, who provide their own endings to their particular stories.

"If I may take the liberty, dear, your story will be tightly scripted, and will not veer far from reality, except in one important detail. But my question to you remains unanswered. Will you choose love or convenience? As my stories reveal, love requires action on your part, and yes, embarrassment. Convenience requires little or nothing from you. For convenience Lady Brighton's actions will do admirably. She will do what is necessary to alleviate an unhappy situation. So what shall it be, alleviation or change? I am giving you a hand in creating your own London Lady story. There is no point in shilly-shallying about the matter. The time for reflection is past. Are you willing to make-do with your philandering husband, and rely on the possibility that he will philander less, or do you wish to marry the man you love?"

"If I only could remarry, if the situation were different, if I could follow my heart —"

"You speak as foolishly as he does. Do you wish to marry the Marquis of Kendall?"

"I do not dispute your vast knowledge of these matters, Lady Maltby, but in this you are mistaken. I wish to marry his handyman, Edward Riley."

"Nonsense. His handyman's name is Phineas McFinch. He has worked on the estate for forty years and he is sixty-five years old. Are we speaking of the same man?"

Julia's shocked expression was her response.

"I thought not. I have spoken to Lord Kendall and he is as confused as you as to how to proceed. He pretended to come into Lord Tilton's employ to avoid the pomp and bother that attends one of his station when what he wants is a pleasant London stay as a normal human being. The young lord's father and Lord Tilton were boyhood friends. I've sent for Edward. He should be here shortly. It was necessary to make him, but not Lord Tilton, as yet, aware of my identity. Meanwhile, on to the plot. Stephen will voluntarily give you a divorce."

"Never."

"He will when I'm through with him. He will refuse to raise as his own a child sired by another man."

"Good heavens! Are you suggesting —"

"Yes, suggesting is the correct word. A London Lady will suggest you are pregnant, in the early stages, belying your svelte appearance. You will refuse to abort and he will refuse to endure the lifelong shame and support due the child, which, rumor will have it, is likely to be a boy, a son, who will inherit his estate. Your condition and his response to it will make an interesting story. No, it will not end in divorce, in the story at least, but Stephen will create the desired ending, for him, for you, for your husband-to-be. I welcome any contribution you wish to make to the story, but the pregnancy is a must. Only this will assure your actual story a happy ending."

"Stephen will insist on confirmation from our physician."

"Dr. Walters will be in Ireland until spring. Our performance will be over long before then."

"There are other medical experts."

"Yes, and the one Stephen will undoubtedly call is Lord Tilton's esteemed physician. Skeleton in the closet. I can handle him."

"Will the truth, the subterfuge be revealed?"

"Not in the story, but in real life, yes."

"He'll be the laughingstock of London. I want a divorce, but I don't want to be a party to his disgrace. I detest his philandering, but I do owe Stephen something. He has supported me in respectable, if not lavish style, for five years. I would feel guilty reducing his status in public opinion. It might even affect his income."

"For the heartache he's caused you he deserves no pity. You are too generous."

"But what will become of him if he allows me a divorce? Family is everything in our circle."

"All right, Julia. If you insist we shall give him one. I have wealthy friends in Paris, a devoted couple with a daughter they are desperate to marry off. She's twenty-nine, nearing old-maid status. No one wants the child. She's no beauty, but decent looking. She complains a lot about almost everything, but married men have endured worse. Stephen will adapt."

"But does she at least have charm?"

"She doesn't need charm. She's got money. When she marries Stephen her money becomes his money. Public knowledge of a married man's sexual liaisons reduces his respectability, but wealth increases it. It balances out."

"What if this young woman refuses to marry Stephen?"

"She would agree to marry the post-boy, if her parents would allow it. Stephen will have no lack of bedtime fun, or exercise after the church bells ring, and probably before."

The cobblestones announced an arrival.

"Ah, Lord Tilton's barouche. Lord Edward has arrived. Do have more tea. I shall greet the lover." Lady Maltby rose and hurried to the door.

"Edward, just in time for tea." She led him to the drawing room.

Edward stood at the entrance gazing in amazement at Julia, as she sat, her teacup in the air, gazing at him. Lady Maltby was vexed.

# MASQUERADE

"This is not a propitious beginning to A London Lady story. Say 'How do you do,' at least."

"Here is the biscuit recipe you asked of Lord Tilton's cook," Edward responded instead.

"Edward, do enter. Conversation at a distance is difficult, and considering the nature of our conversation impossible."

"How are you, Edward," offered Julia.

"Fine. And you?"

Lady Maltby rolled her eyes. "Let's get down to business. Do I rightly assume you are formal with Julia because she is a married woman?"

"It is only proper —"

"And do I correctly assume that if she weren't you would take her in your arms and carry her off to Gretna Green?"

"I dare not even think —"

"Then don't. Feel. We are gathered here together in the sight of Lord Maltby's ancestors hanging on the walls to make this possible."

Edward sat quickly next to Julia. "Oh, would you have me if you could?"

"Yes, she would." answered Lady Maltby impatiently. "I've just been explaining how." And she repeated the conversation of minutes earlier. "I cannot plop a pregnancy in the middle of a story without preparation. The suitor and the young woman must demonstrate their growing affection and love before its culmination. And the husband must indicate a gross appetite the Church of England would roundly condemn. I'll take care of presenting the infidel, but I require inspiration to delineate the mood and affection of the lovers. I want you and Julia to meet often, accidentally it would seem, and devour each other with your eyes, your movements, your words. The story will replicate and build on that. This will take practice. Displaying feelings in public is difficult. An audience does not encourage natural behavior. Thoughts are already crowding my head for your story, but the public must see that it verifies what they have previously seen in your behavior. if you get into the required romantic mood, you will be better able to reflect it, even in the somewhat restrained environment of a crowded street, a solemn dinner, a concert, an art gallery. Are you willing to get into such a mood now?"

Of course they were.

"All right. I am directing this scene-play. Edward, do as follows: Admire her ankles. Good. Now slowly run your hand up her right leg. Stop at her garter. Look at me. Your expression is perfect. Stand up, Julia. Now Edward, run your hands down her arms, and as you do so pull her in closer. Good."

"What do I do, Lady Maltby?"

"Don't stand there like a stick, Julia. Display your heart on your face. Your arms caress his softly, without the vigor his have displayed. Good. Now your hands slowly begin to encircle his neck. Edward, run your hands up her sides, And now across her waist."

"Oh!" exclaimed Julia.

"Edward! Not so high! This is the Maltby mansion, not a bordello. Now softly touch your lips to her cheeks, now her forehead, now down the bridge and top of her nose to her lips."

Julia could no longer restrain laughter, as Edward dutifully followed the Maltby orders. In so doing she parted her lips and Edward's mouth entered hers.

"No, her lips, Edward. You're too soon doing more."

But Edward was oblivious to further demands. He embraced Julia, and her arms encircled his neck. He lifted Julia in his arms and carried her to a distant corner of the drawing room where he put her down and their practice for public events continued.

Lady Maltby's tea was now cold. "I'll brew some more," she announced to the walls. When she returned the lovers were still at it. She reflected that her instructions were unnecessary. Nature had taken over. She would do best sticking to her writing. She lifted the lid on the kettle and steam exploded from the pot. "Too hot," she declared... "I'll get some cream."

# CHAPTER EIGHTEEN

For the next two weeks the young couple met amidst a congregation of street vendors, whose fruit, pastry and coffee they enjoyed in the nearby plaza on a bench that allowed them to see and be seen by the passersby. No one seemed to notice them, but that is the way gossip often begins. They ate, drank, spoke, laughed, and seemed totally relaxed and comfortable. Julia sampled his fare and Edward's hers, but now several hours earlier, when the baker first began calling out his wares and servants buying for their households flocked to purchase before the freshest and the best were gone. Gossip was swift and every breeze carried the dual infidelities of Lord and Lady Langley throughout London. "Which came first?" was the question on everyone's lips, followed immediately by the question "Why?" A London Lady's story was not yet available to answer those questions.

******

"I heard the strangest story from my maid, Julia," said Georgina. She saw you and Edward enjoying breakfast on the plaza at 6 a.m. You're never out of the house that early, and with Edward, a twenty-minute ride from Lord Tilton's, there as well — impossible!"

Julia assured her it was true. "We can no longer speak at mandolin lessons, so we've taken to speaking before our work-day begins."

"Julia, you are treading dangerous ground. The only outcome for such behavior is disaster. Mother is doing her best to ease the pain of being married to a blackguard. What you are doing will only increase it."

"Georgina, you are my dearest friend, so I will tell you this. It is part of a plan, and the parts will get more uncomfortable until I am rid of Stephen."

"Be realistic, Julia. He's yours for life, and it's not such a terrible life if you can school yourself to turn a blind eye to his evenings out. Other women have, other women less intelligent, less kind-hearted, less beautiful than you. You've used your attributes to uplift others, to bring a measure of joy into their lives. You have something to contribute. Stephen's behavior does not affect what you do. Don't let him destroy who you are."

"I will not be destroyed, and I will not be tied in unholy matrimony. Edward and I are putting our hearts and souls into the plan."

"What plan? How can you devise a successful plan for personal happiness when whatever you concoct will unhinge society's mores and leave you, at least, a social outcast? A servant has little to lose. You have a lot."

"By ourselves we cannot, but we have help. And we'll need yours too to support and defend our actions."

"This is madness, Julia. Who is helping you?"

Julia hesitated.

"I swear myself to secrecy, Julia, but I must know who this person is and what the plan is. I cannot advise you otherwise, and I want to, my dearest friend. God forbid you should ruin your life for an unattainable dream."

"A London Lady is guiding us."

Shocked and speechless, it was several minutes before Georgina was able to respond.

"She can create a story to disgrace Stephen, but how can she get you a divorce?"

"I have to pretend I've done something that Stephen cannot endure."

"Stephen is tough material. He can withstand anything except, perhaps, your fathering a child by — No!"

"Yes."

Georgina was once again awestruck.

"I rescind my objection. That will do it if anything can, but the embarrassment for you —"

"In the short-run."

"If you can bear it, I'll help anyway I can. This London Lady — what is she like?"

"Intelligent, kind, moral and determined."

"Thank God someone like that is turning the wheels. However did you meet her?"

"I befriended her."

"You befriended her?"

"I didn't know who she was. I thought she needed kindness."

"And she is now returning the favor. A woman of mystery with a dual identity. Don't tell me who, not yet. I want to savor the expectation you have aroused. What outlandish behavior can I expect from you and Edward in the coming days?"

"More of what your maid reported, an intensification of it."

"You won't regret moving from her ladyship to being a commoner's wife?"

"I was born a commoner, but it won't be necessary to return to that. Edward is the Marquis of Kendall, the late Lord Kendall's son."

Georgina was again struck dumb. Finally — "Pinch me, Julia. I can't believe today is happening, but happening or not, you can rely on my unqualified and absolute support. Is there anything I can do now?"

******

The next month provided food for the gossips that titillated unhappy and bored housewives throughout London. Julia and Edward were seen together at Marble Arch, pressed against it and each other as a violent wind raged through the city. Edward was seen holding Lady Langley's hand as they crossed an icy patch of road caused by an ice wagon spill. He was seen extending his hand to her as he approached her on Bond Street when a passing wagon, tall with goods, blocked them from view for a few seconds. Who knew what went on behind the wagon out of view? The couple were seen strolling in Hyde Park in constant conversation. They were seen daily somewhere in the city. A married Lady and an estate employee. What was going on?

*******

"What is going on, Julia? I cut off your access to this man when I ended your mandolin lessons. Why is there still contact between you?"

"You ended the lessons, Stephen. You said nothing about contact or friendship."

"My meaning was clear. You are to stop seeing this man immediately. No casual contacts or arranged meetings are to take place."

"We only talk, and in public."

"Public places, where people can see and elaborate and spread tales that embarrass me. Cut off your contact with this man immediately. This is an order!" and he strode to the library and shut the door behind him.

Julia mused that the background for A London Lady's story was being successfully set. Soon it would verify the gossip and amplify the fears of an improper relationship. A chill was in the air and Julia went to her bedchamber to retrieve a scarf and a wool bonnet. Her neighborhood stroll was uneventful and strange. She walked alone. It was strange not to have Edward by her side. But he was in her mind and in her heart more than ever. And the plan must continue to — wherever it would lead. The next day she would stay home, awaiting the Tilton carriage and the financial papers that would arrive for Stephen with Lord Tilton's amendments and signature. Julia had been instructed, not the butler or the maid, to hand-deliver them to Stephen upon his return home. Stephen would be late that evening, a business engagement, so he had said. To her surprise he arrived at the usual hour, and in the barouche, and was in no mood for talk or dinner. He entered the house quickly, gave a curt nod to Julia, and slammed himself into the library. It was then that she saw the Tilton carriage arrive, the Earl's crest gleaming in the last rays of the setting sun. Out of the carriage jumped Edward. She waved the butler off and opened the door to greet him. He handed her a thick envelope before the Tilton carriage sped off.

"We had a late start, but Gerald insisted the driver pick up the shawl he ordered for Amy before the shop closes. I hopped aboard because I had to see you. Seeing you in my dreams is not enough, and I wanted to tell you — Let's go inside away from prying eyes."

"Prying eyes are in the kitchen, dining room, breakfast room and drawing room, and Stephen is in the library. And in a huff."

The Langley barouche had not yet been put away. Reggie, beckoned from a window, had hurried in for one of Mrs. North's hot biscuits before putting the vehicle to bed. Edward pointed to it. "Let's talk inside." Julia's mind was in a whirl, and without thinking she allowed his arm to lead her down the walk and help her into the carriage. He raised the cover to conceal them and kissed her passionately.

"Now, darling, there has been a change for the confrontation Lady Maltby has designed. Instead of my accusing Stephen of infidelity before her novella is published, I will do so after that event. Her work, she feels will make the accusations reasonable, whereas before it appears such verbal accusation may lead to a physical altercation, which it is best to avoid. We won't have long to wait. Copies will soon arrive from France. I'll see you soon, my sweet. Another kiss and he backed out of the barouche and was about to lift Julia after him when a sound behind him caused him to turn. He was face to face with Lord Langley.

"What were you doing with my wife in our carriage?"

"Talking, Lord Langley."

"With the cover down?"

"It seemed wiser than conducting our conversation in the street, people might talk, and I know I'm not welcome in your house."

"Do you have your mandolin with you? I'd like to break it over your head."

"No need to destroy an innocent instrument, Lord Langley. Good day."

As he turned away Stephen pulled him around and landed a powerful punch to his chin that slammed him into the barouche. Edward returned the punch and Stephen fell backward, but remained on his feet. Thus began a boxing match on the street, which quickly attracted a crowd, but no interference. In the course of the melee Edward's pocket watch tumbled from his jacket. He quickly retrieved it, and with an exclamation of surprise, turned, jumped aboard the barouche and into the driver's seat and took off down the street. Julia was too choked with anger at Edward's presumption to say a word, even had he been next to her to hear. The barouche stopped a few minutes later, Edward jumped off, waved her a goodbye and climbed aboard the last coach leaving London before it took off on its rounds.

******

Amy Burton was attempting to calm Lord Tilton whose sofa table held the morning newspapers. Their headlines were striking:

THE MORNING CHRONICLE

LORD TILTON SERVANT IN FISTICUFFS WITH LORD LANGLEY, DRIVES OFF WITH HIS WIFE

THE MORNING HERALD
LORD TILTON SERVANT FIGHTS LORD LANGLEY FOR LADY LANGLEY
THE TIMES
STREET BRAWL OVER LADY LANGLEY.
LORD TILTON SERVANT ABDUCTS THE LADY IN HER CARRIAGE

"Why am I dragged into this? Lord Tilton, Lord Tilton, Lord Tilton!" The Earl of Tilton picked up each newspaper and dropped it back onto the table. And he's not my servant! I give him papers to deliver and he gets into a fight with my banker! "

"Darling, he didn't start the fight, and I'm sure he has a reasonable explanation."

Gerald, Lord Tilton slumped back in his chair. "I doubt it. A man in love is never reasonable." He sat erect as Edward entered the room. "Edward, I sent for you two hours ago. Where have you been?"

"At the Maltby mansion, Sir, visiting the old lady."

Lord Tilton softened. "Doing penance for your rash behavior yesterday at the Langley's."

"Actually, I went on a matter of pleasure, but I did suffer a sharp rebuke from that wonderful woman."

"What's been going on at the Maltby mansion? Nothing, I hope that would cause the late mistress of the house to turn over in her grave."

"No, Sir. She couldn't do that even if she wanted to. She's not in it."

"Boy, I was at her funeral seven years ago. She's in it."

"If so, she's the loveliest, liveliest, flesh-and-blood corpse one would ever hope to see."

Lord Tilton, astonished, leaned forward in his chair. "You mean the old woman is taking care of Lady Maltby?"

"No, Sir. The old woman, stripped of her cosmetics IS Lady Maltby. She adores Julia, who, as you know, regularly visits the person she deemed to be an old, lonely woman, and the old, lonely woman wants to help her find happiness. Lord Langley is a blackguard, and unworthy of his precious wife. Lady Maltby sends congratulations to you and Amy on your engagement. She has closely followed Amy's activities and has pronounced her a worthy wife. She likes a kind, moral woman with spunk. 'Just right for my dear, stiff friend Gerald,' she said."

Lord Tilton smiled broadly and clasped Amy's hands. "Eugenia was the makings of Lord Maltby, a wonderful woman and wise counselor all his life. Why did she not reveal herself to me?"

"That's a story for another time, but she invites you, Amy, Georgina, me and Julia to a meeting of The Romantic Conspirators at the mansion tomorrow night at eight."

"It's a wonder she didn't invite A London Lady," joked Lord Tilton, lifting a wine glass to his lips.

"That was not necessary. She is A London Lady."

Lord Tilton's glass flew out of his hands and shattered on the floor.

## CHAPTER NINETEEN

"I must buy this wine, a dozen bottles at least, for my cellar, Eugenia."

"It's my husband-to-be's favorite."

"Heavy, smooth, and what depth! Perfect for the winter months. A marvelous burgundy." Lord Tilton took another draught and sighed with pleasure.

"You've stayed some time in Paris, Amy, have you not?"

"Yes, Lady Maltby. In addition to spices, my husband sold wines from small, overlooked vineyards, more affordable for the less financially endowed. We traveled widely, but I think Paris to be the most beautiful and beautifully laid out city in the world. It's too bad when London burned a century ago that it was not possible to reconfigure the city."

"Yes, and do call me Eugenia. There were too many businesses and set interests that made that impossible. But it's home and always will be, even though Jacque and I will reside in Paris. We'll visit London at least once a year, for The Season. My French is good, but vocal recitals and theatre are for me still best heard in English. You and Gerald must visit us. I'd like our budding friendship to increase. You are my type of friend. And we are looking to purchase a chateau here, in the English countryside. What fun it will be, rebuilding, re-energizing, renewing our interest in the simple pleasures of life - and making a difference. A Paris Lady shall deal with substantial issues for one of my darling's magazines. You can look forward to a similar renewal and purpose, Gerald, with your darling, Amy."

Amy reached for Gerald's hand and squeezed it. He leaned over and kissed her on the cheek.

"But now, my Romantic Conspirators, on to business. My latest book will be available in all the libraries and in stock at all the booksellers very soon. Your preparation for the gossip it will generate must begin now. Julia and Edward — looking at each other with adoration is a given. No further practice, if any was ever needed, is necessary, but you must play the part I've designed for you in other ways. Edward, you must appear somewhat absent-minded and preoccupied in your daily dealings with the other servants. Julia, you must do more., Firstly, you must look the part. For example, you are wearing a lovely dress, but you must begin wearing dresses not so lovely, dresses designed to hide a growing mid-section. Georgina, you've had three children, and Robert is a purveyor of fabrics. Guide her as to what will look best, but create the desired illusion."

"Are you sure I shouldn't tell Robert?"

"No, my dear Georgina. The fewer in on this scheme, the better. Men are not necessarily to be trusted. Robert is a good man, and he is in love with you, but that does not mean he would understand or approve our mission. You needn't look outraged, Gerald. I know you understand and approve because you are more than in love. You are a lover. Lovers can be trusted."

The change in posture of Lord Tilton and the glow on Amy's face were dramatic.

"And Julia, your eating habits must change. Pregnant women, I hear, often develop a liking for particular foods."

"Pickles would be a good start," offered Georgina.

"Then let it be pickles, or another craving of your choice. Your servants will spread the word about your fetish. You must also simulate morning sickness."

"I don't think I would be a good actress, Eugenia."

"Then don't act. Are there any foods you avoid because they give you cramps?"

"Yes."

"Eat them, not daily, but often enough to make the point that a first little Langley is in the offing. Take to your bed at least twice a week. Lock your bedchamber door. You can catch up on your reading undisturbed. So you won't be required to act at all to achieve the effects of pregnancy. Soon people will be aware of a change in Lady Langley, and my book will confirm their suspicions as to what that change is."

"New dresses will take a week to produce, Julia, but I'll give you a few of mine to tide you over. I'm not expecting to increase our brood."

"Excellent, Georgina," said Lady Maltby.

"Is there nothing I can do?" asked Amy.

"Most certainly! You can supervise the dress and behavior of our lovers, make sure things are done in timely fashion, coordinate our drama. I'm in no position to do so. You will be my eyes, my ears and my mouthpiece. You must also praise Julia and deny belief in her new condition. No one will believe you, but there must be a balance of opinions, to give people pause in their judgments, not too much, but enough to stimulate interest in the truth. As the wife-to-be of a distinguished member of the aristocracy who is a dear friend of Lady Langley, it will be considered appropriate to play the role of defender of the accused."

## SONDRA LUGER

"I will have no problem defending my new friend. And I can act." She turned to Gerald. "Not with you, darling. What I say to you and feel for you will always be real." She pressed Gerald's hand.

"Gerald, you will speak in support of your fiancé and your friend."

"Gladly!"

"Shall we have more tea and pastry? The half year I've been spending in London has encouraged me to hone my cooking and baking skills. My darling will be marrying an improved version of the woman he fell in love with. But before we two become one, some time in the new year, we, The Romantic Conspirators have much drama to look forward to. Next week is Covent Garden's Masquerade Ball, following the performance of The Marriage of Figaro. Julia and Edward, you will wear clothes that will catch the eye and set tongues to wagging. If Julia is accompanied by Stephen it will be obvious who she is, but you, Edward, will be a mystery man, and only your brief conversation with Gerald and Amy will hint at your identity. I leave you to determine your apparel for the event and work out the script for your performance, Edward, with your beloved and Amy, your script supervisor. I will be excited to see the results. But no fisticuffs, please. Lord Tilton's influence was able to keep you from jail after your boxing match with Lord Langley. Yes, I know he began it, but justice doesn't always prevail. This is London. And of course Stephen may refuse to come because of the subject matter. We shall see. Now do help me empty these plates of sweets. I don't think I could resist the temptation to eat what remains. In which case I shall appear as pregnant as dear Julia is meant to be!"

# CHAPTER TWENTY

As she glanced out the window Julia was surprised to see Amy coming up the walk. She joyfully greeted her friend, but saw that she was slightly distraught. After a cup of tea to relax her Amy explained her distress. How was she to proceed? She handed Julia a letter she had received from Julia's brother Jonathan. It read as follows:

Dear Amy,

It's wonderful seeing my parents again, but I miss you. My father is knowledgeable about the latest farming methods and will be an important resource as I plan may own estate. He has accompanied me on visits to available acreage within a two to three hour drive of our homestead, and there are several areas where the soil is rich, and the prospects are over water and mountains. When I return to London I hope you will accompany me to see them to decide which you prefer and to meet my parents. I am assuming, I know, but I am hoping if you cannot say yes to my proposal immediately your view of the beautiful land will allow you to consider it seriously. Love can grow where respect and friendship exist, and if you think well of me that is a propitious start. Please write, tell me what you are doing and if you are thinking kindly of me.

In Hope,

Jonathan

"Julia, you know your brother's heart. How can I write so as not to hurt him?"

# MASQUERADE

"There is no way. When you refuse him he will be hurt. I am curious, though. What do you think of my brother?"

"He is a young, energetic man, who would thrill a girl in her twenties, someone younger and more subdued than I."

"He is looking for someone as bold and forthright as himself."

"There may be a power play in a household like that, and possible boredom if two kindred spirits always think along the same lines. His mind has calculated the kind he would like, but his heart may decide differently."

"What was your husband like?"

"He was quiet, analytical, but interested in the arts and new ideas. We had the arts and new ideas in common and complemented each other in the area of personality."

"Did you know the kind of man you wanted before you met him?"

"Yes, I wanted someone bold and brave, who thought as I did, but I married a man whose company I enjoyed and whom I felt comfortable with. I was twenty-five, mature enough to realize he was the husband for me."

"I was only eighteen when I met Stephen, and twenty when we married. I knew I wanted to get married, but didn't determine the particulars until I was married, when it was too late. He was a good catch, I was told, and I believed it myself. I didn't know if another would come along. Five more years and I would have chosen differently. I would have chosen for love."

"Neither did I choose for love, Julia, but as Jonathan wrote, love can grow if all else is in place."

"Do you find Gerald similar to your first husband?"

"He's a more vigorous man, in thoughts and words, and silly in a most endearing way. I shall enjoy being his wife. He's old-fashioned, but willing to learn, he's quiet, but enjoys social gatherings. He's intelligent, kind, generous and — he needs me."

Julia nodded and smiled. "So what will you write Jonathan?"

"This is the draft I penned, but it seems curt."

Julia waved her on to a reading.

Dear Jonathan,

I will always think fondly of you, but I am in love with someone else. You've known me only a short while. Love does not develop that quickly. Someday you will fall in love, your heart will tell you when you do, and do not be surprised if she is not the one your heart envisioned.

With All Good Wishes,

Amy

"To the point, Amy. You have a romantic soul and no-nonsense talk."

Amy laughed. "From my behavior it's hard to guess what's in my heart. Your heart, too, is only visible to your friends. I shall send Jonathan the letter as written. But your romance requires more publicity. Since Lady Maltby wants you and Edward to be seen in the very social and very public venue of Covent Garden, Gerald has obtained two additional box seats to The Marriage of Figaro for tomorrow night. Will Stephen come?"

"No. I can date the beginning of his extra-marital affairs to the beginning of his refusal to see an annual production of The Marriage of Figaro. It used to be a great favorite."

"That's just as well. Then Edward will sit in the box with us, and you will be seen conversing and dancing at the Ball that follows, without fear of Stephen's interference. Lady Maltby is requiring her informants to spread the word more insistently and more graphically about Stephen's affairs. We can't have people thinking you are unfaithful to Stephen without cause. Any more news from Lady Brighton?"

"Only that Stephen now retains only one of his three current paramours. The one he retains is adamant about requiring a replacement before she gives him up. As President of the Women's Society against Prostitution she has covered her tracks well."

"Her marriage must be very unappealing. Lady Maltby is determined that every speck of Stephen's infidelity be exposed. Has he spoken of Edward since their brawl?"

"Only to say that he is disappointed that Lord Tilton keeps him on. I could see he was bursting to say more, but the Earl of Tilton is his best client, and the one he wants potential clients to know trusts his investing expertise. Tonight I will ask Stephen for permission to attend Figaro with you and Gerald, with no mention, of course, of Edward's attendance. But be it yay or nay I'll await your arrival in the barouche. What time shall you come by?"

# CHAPTER TWENTY-ONE

The carriages were lined up on Bow Street, slowly releasing their occupants, who mounted the stairs past the four Doric columns and the statues of Comedy and Tragedy that flanked the entrance to the Theatre Royal, Covent Garden. After the fire it had been rebuilt in 1808, two years before a married Julia had moved to London with her new husband, and two years before this festive night they were about to enjoy, its decor had been enhanced. The improved acoustics now allowed even a whisper to be heard on the sides of the pit and boxes. A thistle, a rose or a shamrock was now in the circle that fronted each box. The Tilton party made its way to the first of the three levels, with the rose their box symbol for the evening. From the arch that framed the stage, painted red draperies caught the eye. Over the arch was the royal arms painted in relief, with laurels and trumpets, other signs of the majestic British Empire. The theater was lit by patent lamps and chandeliers, but now a magnificent chandelier, lit by gas, a new innovation, was the marvel of the circular ceiling, supported by arches and painted to resemble a cupola, divided into squares and surmounted by the figure of an ancient lyre. Julia always marveled at the majesty and luxury of The Theatre Royal, and felt it most deeply when the entertainment, as tonight, was a romantic opera. Gerald and Amy took adjacent seats, but Julia sat by herself on the pale blue seat while Edward stood behind her, instructed by Lady Maltby to remain in that position until the opera began. All those seated in facing boxes were to clearly see the servant behind his lady fair, or to assume as much, and to wonder at the absence of Lord Langley. The London Season of entertainment and gossip was well under way, and if 3,000 people were not in attendance that night the number was close. For most the paper program was unnecessary. They knew the story of a countess married to a man once adoring and loving who was attempting to seduce the fiancé of Figaro, to sample her before her husband.

The lights dimmed and the exuberant overture began. Julia's married situation did not prevent her from enjoying the fictional one on stage. After three hours all would be well. A shamed Count would be brought to heel. Would that her situation could be as quickly resolved, she mused. Ah, the wooing gallant Stephen had once been when he persuaded her to marry him! "Dove Sono?" Where had those happy days gone "Dove Sono?" sang the Countess. It was an aria Julia loved and knew well. It was the first piece she had asked Edward to teach her on the mandolin. As the Countess sang the lovely, plaintive air, Julia nodded in agreement.

> "Where have the lovely moments of gentleness and pleasure gone?
> What happened to the promises that came from those lying lips?
> If everything has turned to tears and sorrow why have my memories of that happiness not died?
> Dove sono?
> My love is as faithful as ever.
> If only it could give me some hope of changing his heart."

"Yes," thought Julia. "But though I can forgive Stephen and think kindly of him, I can no longer live with him. His infidelity has created a void in my heart. And Edward has filled it."

The garden scene that ends the opera always pleased Julia. The Countess masquerading as Suzanna, whom the Count plans to violate, exposes the Count's intentions to his humiliation. The Count, one assumes, reforms and becomes a devoted husband and Suzanna and Figaro can marry and live happily thereafter. The applause for the performers was long and well deserved.

As most of the audience began their departure, some kept their seats. Several hundred would soon descend on the stage for a masquerade of their own in celebration of this beloved opera. Georgina and Robert left their box to join the Tilton party in theirs, waiting for the House to clear and the stage to be prepared for the influx of celebrants and dancers.

Julia turned to her friends. "I don't think I should make such a spectacle of myself. This may be going too far."

"If you don't go far," said Amy, "you won't get far. Lady Maltby made it clear that your performance on stage was crucial, that the ton must witness you with Edward, talking, laughing, dancing. There will be no country dances tonight. They would not suit the opera. More intimate dances are expected, some minuets and lots of waltzes, we've been told. You and Edward will have ample opportunity to display your affection for each other — and you must!"

Edward, silent all the while, only his eyes revealing his adoration and hope, clasped Julia's hands in his, and this decided her.

"I have no mask," Julia offered weakly.

"Lady Maltby thought it best not to frighten you. She anticipated your doubts." Amy opened her reticule to reveal Julia's mask. "Hand-made by your fairy godmother." Above the yellow glitter that covered the mask was a sparkling red heart. It matched the one on Edward's mask. "As you dance together the meaning will be clear."

"Amy, I will be violating more than my conscience this night. A married woman does not dance with an unmarried man."

"Neither do married or nearly married couples, but Gerald and I will dance together, and happily so."

"Robert and I will do the same," said Georgina.

## MASQUERADE

Julia sighed. "I am outnumbered and outvoted."

The House was nearly empty now, and the musicians began playing themes from the opera as the stage began to fill. Some wore costumes in tune with the opera just ended and some wore elegant evening wear and masks adorned with fruit, feathers, flowers and the like. But the obvious standouts in this assemblage were two young, literally sparkling people, holding hands and chatting as the dance music began. The minuet was superseded by the gavotte, and supplemented by the champagne and pastry continually replaced on the tables that dotted the stage, reddened the cheeks and loosened the tongues and heightened the laughter that bounced off the walls and back onto the stage of the Theatre Royal, Covent Garden. Then the orchestra began playing a waltz, a daring act, but the now inebriated and semi-inebriated were in a daring mood. Julia and Edward had drunk moderately, but they not unwillingly entered into the mood and the dance that the clergy had roundly condemned. Some couples danced holding each other at arm's length, but some held their partners close. Julia and Edward held each other so close they seemed as one, the hearts topping their masks nearly intertwined. Gerald and Amy and Robert and Georgina held each other at a moderate distance.

"If I didn't want to overshadow the effect to be made by Julia and Edward, Amy, I would hold you so close to my heart we would appear to be one." said Gerald.

"We could hide behind that tree," suggested Amy, and for some seconds they did.

When they vacated the space behind the tree, Georgina urged Robert to emulate the pair, but when they parted from the tree they were unable to release themselves from their embrace. A button from Georgina's gown had gotten tangled on one on Robert's suit. Laughter and merriment ensued as other dancers attempted to extricate the pair from their dilemma. Dances alternated between the stately and the seductive, and conversation, unfettered and free, music, magic and mystery wrapped and unwrapped, ambrosial, sweet and bittersweet, played on through the night, a lifetime lived in hours. The theatre bells alerted them that the sun was rising and the festive evening was coming to an end. Gerald and Amy would return home to contemplate their marriage, Robert and Georgina to the comfort of their children and Julia to a problem unresolved and teetering, if all did not go well, on disaster.

It was 3 a.m. Julia would sleep late. She would not see Stephen at breakfast, and that was a consolation. The pleasures of the night could continue before Stephen would be aware that Edward would not relinquish his wife, and that Julia would not want him to. Julia bid a joyous goodbye to her friends, waving happily to Georgina and Robert as their carriage separated from Lord Tilton's, and embracing Amy and Gerald as their carriage reached her house before, with the coachman's assistance, gingerly stepping down and walking to her door. Her dear friends made sure she was safely inside before departing. Julia had told the servants not to wait up for her. It was unconscionable for them to lose sleep because she was off for an evening of entertainment. As she put away her wrap her hand brushed against Stephen's warm winter jacket. As a paper fell from one of its pockets, the note opened and lay before her.

"Come tonight if you can. Mr. M will be away. The entire night will be ours." It was dated the day that was just past. Stephen's elegant jacket was gone. He had worn that instead of the more practical jacket for his rendezvous. Stephen had had his own entertainment that night. She hurried to the side window. The Langley barouche was gone. His entertainment was still underway. She took the candle awaiting her and slowly climbed the stairs to her bedchamber.

# CHAPTER TWENTY-TWO

The morning seemed like any other, as did the morning after, but beyond the walls of the Langley house much was going on. Along with the shopkeepers opening for business and peddlers and tradesmen calling out their wares, and the streets alive with people and horses moving hither and yon for purposes unknown, word was spreading with the speed of a tornado about a certain couple seen in a certain place doing certain things one would not expect unless one expected the scandalous. This news, flying in the wind, brushed against news of salacious doings in private by an eminent banker. The buzz was so loud and so insistent that when Julia left the house to mail some letters to her parents and her brother, she was subjected to smirking smiles, knowing nods and impertinent stares. She extended the collar of her coat as high as it would go and pulled it closer to her face. What were people saying about her and Stephen? She wanted to know. When the footman returned from shoeing the horse, and Maggie returned from shopping, and the upstairs and downstairs maids returned with the voluminous fabrics she had ordered, and the cook returned with the spices required for the evening meal, and the butler returned from lunch at the tavern, she called a meeting of the household staff and asked them. Their fear and trepidation was evident, but Julia assured them there was no need for it. She wanted and could withstand the truth.

 * "The buzz about Lord Langley's night life has grown louder. There is no surprise at it. Bankers have a reputation for scandalous behavior away from home. The surprise is at your behavior, Lady Langley. Some are disappointed that you have not risen above his

# MASQUERADE

behavior, and some welcome that you have taken revenge of it." The butler bowed and stepped back.

* "London ladies think fondly of you, and most insist there is no proof of your moral decline. The Tilton staff would know, the shopkeepers would know, we would know. Appearances prove nothing, but all agree the appearances are troubling." Maggie curtsied.

* "No one was surprised that you and the Tilton servant sat in his box, but most were surprised at the absence of Lord Langley. Some knowledgeable about the opera said that the subject matter kept him away, feelings of guilt overriding interest in the opera and dance to follow. But some said Lord Langley's permission in allowing you to attend showed he had no fear of your behavior." Edna smiled bravely and was silent.

* "Others said he should have had fear after Tilton's man abducted you in the barouche," Mrs. North said stoutly.

* Julia's gaze rested on Reggie. "No one spoke kindly of your behavior at the ball after the opera. Pardon me, your ladyship, but it was thought to be bold, brazen and inappropriate for a lady of your estate and reputation."

* The butler moved forward. "In sum, your ladyship, there are conflicting views about events, behaviors and reasons for them, but the majority of the women retain their respect and appreciation of your kindly self and the suspicions about Lord Langley's behavior. The men generally keep their affection for you and silence on the widespread rumors concerning the master. The women attribute this to solidarity of the sex. That is all m'lady. You did ask."

"And it is quite enough, Jameson! And yes, I did. Have no fear. You are all still engaged here. I appreciate your honesty and your service."

# MASQUERADE

Hot on the heels of gossip unveiled came an unmistakable knock on the door. It was the firm, demanding knock of Lady Brighton. Jameson showed her in and escorted her to the library to which Julia had repaired. Lady Brighton locked the door and faced her.

"Thanks to my intervention Stephen was denied the company of his mistress of last night. What a pity, though, that threats, rather than morality have so salutary an effect on miscreants. A new one, Mrs. M was brought to heel."

"No wonder Stephen came home early yesterday, and in a huff. Pleasure was denied him. Aunt Margaret, it is impossible to stanch the flood of mistresses that Stephen can have access to. I mustn't allow you to fight my battles, especially when the war cannot be won. I appreciate your love, but this is asking too much of it."

"Then you will be content to make your peace with this male aberration?"

"Not exactly. Have you not heard of my daring behavior of two nights past?"

"Oh, that. We know why Stephen didn't attend. You're entitled to nights out without him in the company of respected friends."

"Thank you, dear Margaret, and there is more of that to come. I pray you will support me. You recall that you said jealousy was a way to arouse Stephen's ardor."

"What are you planning, Julia?"

"The plan is not mine, but its execution is, with the help of Edward Riley. It involves disgrace, dear Margaret, terrible disgrace to achieve its goal. The rumor mill must move into high gear once more. Stephen wants a child — "

"No, Julia, you mustn't!"

"I won't. Only the appearance of scandal is necessary."

"if Stephen thinks you are siring Edward's child he will divorce you, is that the plan?"

"It is."

"Rubbish! And what brilliant mind concocted this plan?"

"Your old nemesis, Eugenia Maltby."

"So you won't tell me, your staunchest supporter and friend?"

"I have told you, dear Margaret."

"From the grave Eugenia's ghost returns to vex me?"

"From the Maltby mansion. Like Stephen, me and Edward she is involved in a masquerade. Ours will ultimately be revealed, hers perhaps never."

Lady Brighton gazed in wonder at Julia. "Lady Maltby alive? Well, if anyone could escape death she could, a worthy opponent and an admirable wife."

"She has a high regard for you as well, Margaret."

"I must see her!"

"She's expecting you."

"She's probably engaged A London Lady to stamp approval of her scheme."

Julia smiled, her eyebrows raised.

"Oh, no, don't tell me!" She laughed uproariously. "An amazing woman!"

******

Lady Maltby opened the door, and she and Lady Brighton embraced.

"We've finally found a common bond. What took us so long?"

"Destructive pride. Do join me in the kitchen, Margaret. My chocolate soufflé is almost ready. I've become an excellent baker since my death."

The women chatted as though they had been friends all their lives. The usually vocal Lady Brighton listened in wonder to what Lady Maltby had been up to for seven years. Lady Maltby knew all about her new friend's secret actions, her informants having supplied her with details.

"Has no one questioned Stephen about his night-time absences and the rumors?"

"Julia has, Eugenia. He denies the rumors and pleads business. I have avoided the subject. Interfering aunts are not likely to hear the truth and less likely to be welcome visitors to the home."

"Perhaps it's time to take the risk and speak to Stephen about the matter. You can assert fear that your sister's son is allowing gossip to taint his reputation, and that Julia should not be subjected to innuendos that tarnish you both."

"That would be an encouragement for him to lie and ask my advice on how to counter it."

"You are right. A neutral approach is best."

"That, too, is difficult. He knows I adore Julia, and that I know she questions his behavior to the point of wanting a divorce. I can't admit I know the truth and have been acting on it on her behalf."

"Why not? Other men have fallen, admitted the truth and repented."

"Stephen is not other men. I think he would prefer professing innocence rather than admitting that he lied to Julia."

"You know him best, Margaret. But if he can be persuaded to convict himself, the novella, which will be in bookstores shortly, may deepen the condemnation and persuade him to free Julia and free himself of raising a bastard child."

"Pride will not allow my nephew to convict himself of anything detrimental to his self-esteem and his clients' opinion of him. He is Lord Langley in name only. All his life he has resented being a second son who inherits nothing. He rarely visits or writes to his father, except when he requires funds for some venture, and his father responds out of guilt for having him second. Neither father nor brother was invited to his wedding, and neither was seen often even before as Stephen struggled to achieve success on his own."

"And he has."

"The need to do so still rankles, and the possibility of imminent loss of all he has gained looms large in his psyche."

"How do you think Stephen will react to my novella?"

"That is a mystery to me. I know him well, but not well enough to foresee his reaction to the scathing plot and its resolution. On second thought, Eugenia, I think I should speak to him about the rift between him and Julia. He is family. I shall say —"

******

"Stephen, the rumors swirling about you are upsetting. Can I help you in any way?"

"Thank you, Aunt Margaret, I wish you would, I wish you could. But how do you counter rubbish so widely believed?"

"Much may have been made out of little. Have you, perhaps inadvertently, allowed a woman to —"

"Seduce me? Aunt Margaret!"

"It has happened to good men. Your uncle was not immune to the charms of aggressive women, and your poor Aunt Margaret had to cope with the reality for a time."

"Oh, dear aunt. I didn't know. What caused him to desist?"

"Gout. Stemming the pain took precedence over achieving the pleasure."

"But you seemed so happy."

"We were. Every marriage has its trials."

Stephen strode the length of the morning room before facing his aunt sitting on the sofa, her hands folded. "I can't deny that women have tried to tempt me, lonely women, tied to old or bedridden or negligent husbands who did not appreciate them. My heart broke for them, but I could not be unfaithful to Julia."

"Perhaps a kiss, an embrace in solidarity with their grief?"

"Perhaps, but certainly nothing more. Julia's friendship with Edward Riley is more a blight on our marriage, and a more public one, than anything I have done. Julia adores you. See if you can get her to think more critically of the rumors and more kindly of her husband's behavior." He kissed his aunt farewell. "I shall give Julia your love when she returns from her good samaritan rounds." He escorted her to her waiting carriage and watched as it took off.

Lady Brighton leaned back in her seat and sighed. In a male autocracy seeming misbehavior of a wife is more reprehensible than actual misbehavior of a husband. Power has its privileges that ancillary beings to that power do not possess. If Stephen stopped philandering that should be enough to satisfy Julia, but that Stephen was not willing to do, at least at this time. She wondered how she would have reacted to Lord Brighton's misbehavior if gout had not prevented its continuance. She could afford him the luxury of forgiveness, especially now that he was dead. If Eugenia's novel could effect the divorce that Julia desired it would be a miracle — and for the best. As a single man Stephen could continue his night-time activities on a more moral plane, offending one person less, and Julia could find happiness with a titled man who loves her, and she, a tired Lady Brighton, could cease her detective work and her moral harangues to foolish wives and enjoy her senior years. Despite Julia's request that she cease her moral mission, she could not do so while Julia was unhappy. She sighed and closed her eyes as the carriage tumbled her home.

# CHAPTER TWENTY-THREE

Lady Willie flew through the door, nearly knocking down Jameson who hurried to the breakfast room to announce her to Lady Langley.

"Julia, it's here! It's in the bookshops, dozens of copies in the windows, and a line down the block outside our library. You're a star!"

They both burst into laughter, but sobered quickly as the butler announced Amy Burton. "Ladies, what a morning! I go weekly to my library when it opens. I like a calm atmosphere and to be one of the first to see their latest holdings. Today at this early hour there were two dozen women ahead of me waiting, they said, to borrow A London Lady's latest exposé or be next in line on the list. I passed several bookshops on the way here. Their windows shout A London Lady from one end to the other. Her novellas are always prominently displayed, but not with the thunder accorded this one."

"The rumors have been persistent," said Georgina, "that this time aristocrats will be in the stocks."

"Yes, perfect for our cause, but frightening. Eugenia gave me an advance copy, and I told Gerald to keep a copy of the novella near his person when he sees Stephen on business this morning. He will tell him that he bought it for me at my request, and that thumbing through the book he saw a Lord and Lady Bangley in print, and unfavorably so. He will offer Stephen loan of the copy to see what dastardly business A London Lady is up to in her latest exposé. Julia, I'm worried. Eugenia's idea seemed rational when she espoused it, but it may not meet with a rational reaction from Stephen. Her past tomes have taken the high moral road, but with you she feels personally invested in the matter, and if the road is too high with Stephen his empty title may result in his inability to afford a divorce. Some of his clients may decamp faster than a winter storm if his morals are severely questioned. If the men are reluctant to abandon him, their wives may insist otherwise."

"I was afraid of that too, Amy, but suspicions have been rife for months, and our finances have not been affected."

"Yes, Julia, but they haven't been in print. Talk flies hither and yon, but print strikes you in the eye with a solidity that talk cannot match. Stephen has risen to a position of respect and emolument in the financial community. What took him years to accomplish can be wiped away in an instant. Julia, you may be in danger."

"Amy, I'm sure Eugenia has made it clear that his behavior was more reprehensible than mine, and Stephen has never been violent with me, either physically or verbally."

"What will strike him forcibly will be her depiction of him, not you, and he's never been faced with a potential financial disaster like this."

"Lady Maltby assured me — "

"From behind her nom de plume — "

Georgina turned pale. "Julia, come home with me. Stay with us until we see how Stephen reacts."

"Half of London can't read!" Julia exclaimed defensively.

"But you know a favorite evening past-time is having books read aloud to the family," countered Amy.

"Julia, our carriage will return in an hour. Stay with us," insisted Georgina. "If Stephen behaves badly it will be too late!"

# MASQUERADE

"We can find out how he will behave before he returns home," said Amy firmly. "Julia, your notepaper and a pen."

The women hurried to the library desk. Amy marched up and down the room before she faced Julia, who had pen in hand, and dictated as follows:

Dear Stephen,

A catastrophe has befallen us! A London Lady has heaped dirt upon our names and accused us of the most immoral behavior! Georgina and Amy have heard the worst, and they have been unable to calm my beating heart and my fears. Why should such horror and grief be heaped upon us? What shall we do?

Julia

Julia sealed the note, called for Reggie, and requested immediate delivery to Lord Langley at the bank.

"Now," said Amy. "We will find out what he shall do."

******

"Shocking! A nobody with no name heats up her income by scalding her betters. And my poor Julia! What can this infidel have against my lovely wife, the adoration of all London! That must be what vexes her. Does Julia deserve such treatment, do I?" begged Stephen of Lord Tilton.

"Of course not, Stephen. Such scandalous accusations, and without a jot of proof."

"May I keep this copy, Gerald, I'll pay you — "

"No, no, Stephen. Keep it. Amy will be the better without it. This goes far beyond what the authoress has written in the past!"

"Some jealous woman — or man, who knows. I cannot allow this to stand. The Langley reputation cannot be desecrated in this way."

"But what can you do? The author is unknown. Think no more of it. The next volume in this scandalous series will cast this one in the shadows. It will soon be forgotten. Do not let it plunge you into despair. Your clients depend on your sagacity and attention to their needs."

"Clients are fickle, Gerald. What if I lose them before this debacle subsides? No, I must take action immediately to counter these accusations." He rang for his assistant. "Jeremy, cancel my appointments for today. I am not to be disturbed by anyone." He turned to Gerald. "Thank you for alerting me to this disaster. I will read this vile volume and take notes of the activities of which this Lord and Lady Bangley are accused."

"To what avail?"

"To make known to Beaton, Barton and Bradley the details of the case to bring against this infamous author. And I know just the agents to discover and apprehend the swine. The London Liar will be in the poorhouse before I'm through with her!"

******

Amy and Georgina were still with their friend when the missive arrived. The women huddled over the note as Julia clutched her head.

# MASQUERADE

Dearest,

Fear not. All will be made right. An advertisement will appear in THE TIMES commanding A London Lady to shed her cowardice and reveal her identity. Libel under the guise of anonymity will not be tolerated. The reprobate will undoubtedly not reveal herself, but an amazing duo will discover her identity and the best law firm in the country will indite her and take every pence and shilling she's got for the scandalous, libelous accusations she so nonchalantly hurls at her betters. This shamed, vindictive woman will have all the leisure in the world to write her disgusting novels as she rots in prison. Fear not my love, I will avenge this attack on our reputations and the Langley name.

Stephen

"But what A London Lady accuses him of is accurate," said Amy, "and as for you, Julia, this is a work of fiction."

"My God, Julia," said Georgina, "I know the duo he will undoubtedly hire. They'll turn the city upside down, the country if necessary, to find their prey. Lady Maltby must be warned."

"I'll do that," said Amy. "I think you'll be safe here, Julia. Georgina will give me a lift to the Maltby mansion and on the way back drop off a note to Gerald requesting a carriage there in two hours, which I will spend in high conclave with a certain old woman."

******

Carriage wheels were heard outside the mansion, and Gerald, Lord Tilton hurried to the door with a "no, no," to the butler who was about to do the same. But it was not Amy returning for a private dinner with him. He faced instead, a menacing Stephen, Lord Langley.

"Good evening, Gerald. I've come to see Edward Riley. Where can I speak with him in private."

"Don't do anything rash, Stephen. It will only make matters worse."

"What I intend to do is talk, Gerald, nothing more."

Lord Tilton instructed the butler to summon Edward. An interminable silence later Edward Riley appeared, and Lord Tilton escorted the men to his study, and with warning glances at them both, parted from them. He motioned to two male servants working nearby and ordered them to stand guard outside the study door and enter at the first audible sign of violence.

"Mr. Riley, have you read THE FALLEN ARISTOCRAT?"

"No, Lord Langley, but its contents have been buzzed about."

"Is it fact or fiction?"

"I have no knowledge of whether the depiction resembling you is accurate, m'lord."

"I am speaking of the aristocrat's wife and her fictional lover."

"You have answered the question, m'lord. It is fiction."

"Why have you pursued my wife these two months?"

"It has been friendship, not pursuit. The story an anonymous writer chooses to manufacture out of it is beyond my ability to restrain."

"Why would she manufacture an untruth?"

"Only she can answer that. My assumption is that it attracts readers and financial largess. The wealthy are fair game for distortion in the eyes of those of lesser social estate."

"Your proximity to my wife on multiple occasions has been recorded in the gossip of multiple servants. If you are truly her friend why do you continue your visible friendship when you must know it will subject her to talk detrimental to her character?"

"I cannot allow my friendships to be determined by household help and envious spectators."

"Are you having an affair with my wife?"

"I am not. Lady Langley is a virtuous woman respected by all of sound mind."

"I want you to cease your visible friendship with my wife. You may continue your friendship in letters, though the less of those the better. Servants are aware of everything. When do you return to your position at Kendall Hall?"

"Soon."

"When is soon — a month, three months, a year?"

"A month."

"Good. Stay away from my wife until then. You may speak your farewells in my presence. Do you agree?"

"I agree."

"Good. Now I have only to deal with A London Lady."

"You know who she is?"

"Not yet, but her identity shall not be hidden from me for long." Stephen put his hand on the doorknob, but turned and met the eyes of Edward Riley. "Are you in love with my wife?"

"Yes, I am."

Lord Langley turned away, opened the door and left the study. He walked briskly to the entrance and made his exit without a farewell to his host, who was only aware of his departure by the sound of horses' hoofs carrying him away.

\*\*\*\*\*\*

Stephen arrived home later than usual. This time Julia knew another woman was not responsible for the delay. The moment she dreaded had arrived. Stephen did not speak. He motioned her to the library, closed the door and locked it. A slight shiver enveloped her body, but she was quickly in command of herself when he faced her in front of the section housing the legal books. She pointed to the sofa and they sat. Anger was less likely and more controllable, she thought, seated.

"Have you read THE FALLEN ARISTOCRAT?"

"I have not, but I have received a graphic description of its contents."

"Are you having an affair with Edward Riley?"

"Of course not. I'll be glad to swear on a Bible. Have you engaged in liaisons with other women?"

"Of course not. So we are both innocent victims of this writer of salacious romances. You know I trust you, but I had to ask. Our good reputations will soon be restored. My note this afternoon explained how. But I am dismayed you did not obey my request to stop seeing Edward Riley. Had you done so, the affair imagined by the writer would not be in print. Why did you disregard my order?"

"I am your wife, not a servant. I have caused you no shame and do not think your order fitting for your station or my character."

"Now that we are subjects of scandal will you do so?"

"Yes, Stephen. There is sense to it now."

"What is so special about this man's friendship? He is hardly likely to rise above his current economic or social state."

"He is a man of character and varied interests. He has a sunny personality and a charming laugh."

"Are you in love with him?"

Julia hesitated before she spoke. "I am a dutiful wife. I do you credit in all the venues you traverse. I am entitled to some privacy. I do not choose to share the contents of my heart. I am tired. This has been a day like no other. Please excuse me, but I wish to retire."

She rose, walked to the library door and unlocked it. Stephen watched her leave and heard the boards creaking on the third and fourth staircase steps as she ascended to her bedchamber.

# CHAPTER TWENTY-FOUR

The men at Boodles couldn't stop slapping him on the back and plying him with scotch and soda, laughing heartily at the mention of A London Lady. The humor of his situation eluded Stephen. Was it because it freshened the banal, boring topics that were the mainstay of conversation at the club, or was it because they were grateful they were not the subject of the scandal emanating from this writer's pen? What are you going to do now, how are you going to cope was the eagerly asked question, asked in a way that displayed disbelief that there was anything he could do but enjoy the ride of notoriety. Old Lord Wexler abstained from the merriment.

"You haven't escaped Stephen, my boy, but why drag your saintly wife through the mud? A nasty disposition has that London Lady, no lady at all to cast your wife to the wolves while denigrating you. Julia's name will ultimately be cleared, has to be. It's beyond belief the evidence will support the vindictive writer's accusations. But you are another story. How will you clear your reputation, lad? That evidence cannot create itself, but somehow it must if you are to prove your innocence."

"Gossip is not evidence. Fiction is not evidence. I deny all wrong-doing. Julia will vouch for my innocence." Stephen stared defiantly at Lord Wexler across two rows of scotch.

"That would carry weight. Has she said she will do it?"

"She will do it. Our lives, our reputations are one. I love Julia. Who doesn't? She's admired for her affability, her concern for others and her honesty, as well as her beauty. We will weather this debacle."

"In my old age I have nothing to occupy my time but to enjoy the foolishness of my neighbors and, of course, my whisky. Our servants know more about us than we do, their judgments can be trusted, its spread surreptitious but clear for all to hear."

"What they say is in the undertow. What a wife says carries heavy weight."

"Have you promised what a wife like yours wants to hear, or do you expect compliance with your request for defense in defiance of your continuing behavior?"

"I've admitted nothing. She will trust my word."

"For your sake I hope she will. For her sake I hope you will desist from disgracing her." He put up both hands to ward off the denial. "I was young once. I've been through it all. Why do you continue, Stephen?"

A half-dozen lies were about to issue from Stephen's lips, but staring into Lord Wexler's faded blue eyes he knew the old man could not be deceived. He had always admired him for that, but now it was inconvenient and embarrassing.

"The truth, man."

"It is hard to be a saint when fortune has denied a man the land and power that provide him with respect and privileges. He must gain as much as he can of both by hard work and determination, and he grasps whatever he can of both outside his home. Admiration and respect from family is of lesser quality. It is expected. You were born into privilege, Lord Wexler. You have not experienced the disregard and lesser status of a second-tier son. No matter how hard I work, how much I achieve, my rank can never attain the regard and respect that you enjoy."

"Self-regard trumps the world's, my boy. Do you not feel the difference? Infidelity is a selfish, addictive habit, but you can break it."

"It is not totally selfish, Lord Wexler. Meeting the needs of others less fortunate, less blessed with happiness is entwined in this habit. You know that marriage is a woman's only hope for a comfortable life. Affection is a negligible consideration in forming a union. Meeting the needs of an unhappy woman who must seek an outlet for the frustrations she must endure in a loveless marriage is not a small thing."

Lord Wexler looked at Lord Langley in amazement. "Are you saying you are doing a public service by bedding these women?"

"It does ease the pain in their existence."

"What about the pain this causes in Julia's existence? Is your wife of lesser importance than a world of women who acceded to their fate, unhappily or not?"

"Of course not, but I am not alone in feeling an obligation to increase the happiness of others in this way."

"I thought I knew you well, Stephen, but you astonish me. Are your morals contingent on following the immorality of other men?"

"You mistake my meaning. I will make an effort to accord my wife more of the attention and love she deserves, but you know I am not alone in this."

"Continue in this demeaning behavior and you will be alone. A London Lady has shown your wife the way to freedom and to your everlasting disgrace."

"I will never divorce Julia. She is the crowning joy of my life. I would never raise a bastard son in the ludicrous scenario suggested by a demented writer. I will make an effort to please my wife."

## MASQUERADE

"You will have to do better than that to keep Julia happy and provide yourself with the opportunity to sire a proper son. I'd wager your behavior has kept her from doing just that. You must realize what this fiction that is selling out in all the bookshops may cost you. The remuneration for your services, highly regarded as they are, may suffer, as clients, suspicious of your moral conduct, go elsewhere. Reconsider what you are doing to your wife, your income and your reputation."

"You have the wisdom of years, Lord Wexler, and I appreciate your sharing it with me."

"Hardly wisdom, Stephen, common sense."

"You will keep this conversation private."

"You know I will. Poor Julia, she will suffer, but the novelist cannot destroy her reputation. I don't think she meant to. She will emerge from this work unscathed. Your reputation, I fear, will not fare as well. You face an uphill battle to convince London of your moral rectitude. You haven't much, but that doesn't mean you can't convince most of the world that you have. Barring threatening a duel to declare your innocence, I don't know what you can do."

Stephen was silent for a moment. "A duel," he murmured, stroking his chin. "I was fencing champion at college, and pistol champion as well. If Edward Riley is made aware of my talents, he would be a fool to accept a challenge to duel."

"What if he were fool enough to accept it?"

"I would win. I don't think he could defeat me with a mandolin. My challenge would proclaim my innocence and put rumor to rest."

"Don't do it, Stephen. The outcome is not guaranteed."

"I will take your advice, my friend."

"Which piece of advice?"

Stephen's response was an unsettling smile.

******

Edward Riley stared at the note before him. It read —

You have dishonored the Langley name. Your pursuit of my wife has encouraged a writer of fiction to amplify this scandalous, unwarranted dishonor. If you do not cease your unwelcome attentions to Lady Langley and leave London within a week I propose to end your slanderous behavior in a duel on December 10, 1815 at Hyde Park on the lawn adjacent the Promenade at noon. Depart London before then or be there.

Lord Langley

Lord Tilton looked curiously at his friend. "What is it, Edward?"

Edward lifted the note which rested on the Tilton account books and passed it to him.

"This is madness — or desperation or both. You will leave, of course. Lady Maltby's plot can be continued at a distance."

"I will not leave. Lord Langley is the cause of his own disgrace. Lady Maltby's plot should soon bear fruit."

"Not within a week, if ever, and a dead suitor will be of no use to Julia and bring no joy to a defunct you."

"Come to the Kendall mansion and you will see my trophies for fencing and artillery in university."

"Stephen has them too. You are as mad as he is. Lady Maltby is clever, without doubt, but cleverness does not guarantee success when dealing with a man determined to disprove the truth and salvage his name and his profession. He can easily disprove Julia's pregnancy with a physician's physical examination, and should she actually be found to be pregnant, yes we know she is not, he can require her to abort and force her to provide him with a proper heir. He was an unrelentingly determined child and this note shows he is even more so as an adult."

"My fleeing from a duel will heap disgrace upon me and corroborate Julia's complicity in a heinous, immoral act."

He roughly grabbed a sheet of writing paper on the desk and spoke as he wrote —

"I will not flee. At noon then on December 10."

He quickly addressed and sealed the letter, rang for a servant and demanded immediate delivery to the Langley residence.

Lord Tilton was astonished at this demand by a young man who was merely a guest in his house, but the look in Edward's eyes kept him silent.

Edward pointed to the account books. "May we continue this in an hour, Gerald?"

"Of course, my boy, calm yourself, go for a walk."

"Edward made a prompt exit, not saying what he would do."

"Lord, help!" whispered Lord Tilton, as he reached for a Bible on a nearby table.

******

Julia was besides herself. "You'll be killed, Stephen! How could you do such a foolish thing?"

"I cannot allow my reputation, my wife, my life to be destroyed."

"They will vanish in a flash if you die. Edward Riley is accomplished in the martial arts."

"So am I, but if I die, I die. We will both soon be in the poorhouse if this scandal continues. If my parents had seen fit to have me first, my future would still be bright, and my lazy brother would have to grovel for his bread. Stay home tomorrow, Julia. It is too soon to be seen in public after the onslaught of this smear campaign. Will you do as I say?"

"Yes, Stephen, but it will be seen as fear or shame to be about."

"I don't want you about!" Stephen abruptly left the room and slammed the door behind him.

Julia sank back on the sofa. She rang for the downstairs maid.

"A pot of tea, Maggie, and a plate of buttered crumpets."

"Yes, m'lady. Shall I tell Mrs. North to make more? They're Dr. Walters' favorites."

"I'm well, Maggie. I haven't sent for Dr. Walters. And he's in Ireland for yet another three months visiting family."

"Oh, but he's back, and Reggie delivered a note to him not more than an hour ago, so I thought — I'm glad you're well, m'lady." She curtsied and left for the kitchen.

Julia sighed. Dr. Walters would vouch for her rectitude, but that would not get her a divorce.

******

Julia saw him from the drawing room window and sat resigned as he was ushered in.

"Dr. Walters, what a pleasure to see you when I'm feeling well. You have abandoned your relatives sooner than expected."

"The hospital begged for my return. St. Bartholomew's has been inundated. The influx of people into London from Spain and

## MASQUERADE

France, many unemployed and ill, has kept them busy, and nothing would do but to have Dr. Isaiah Walters lead the wellness charge. I'm not immune to flattery. And my conscience would not allow me to refuse. I barely have time for my private patients now. Stephen suspects a little Langley is on the way. We shall see if he is correct." Jullia escorted him to her bedchamber and he began his examination. At last he returned his tools to their case.

"I am sorry to disappoint Stephen, but no Langley is forming at the present time. You are not disappointed, Julia?"

"No, and neither will Stephen be."

"Testing the fiction of A London Lady, is he? Busy as I am, even I have heard about her. It is never wise to judge one's mate by rumor and fiction."

"In this case I wish he would."

"It pains me to hear it. You married young, not in years, but in experience, but do not let happiness elude you. You are a creative woman, and must and can create your own happiness, just not A London Lady way. That uphill climb would exhaust you, age your lovely features long before their time and require you to see me for far more than a routine examination. There is much to be gained from marriage, even if the marital choice is wrong. You chose too early. I never chose at all. You have a comfortable home life. I have none. My patients have become my family. I couldn't decide which lovely to marry, so I chose none. It is a risk I should have taken. We both have had to live with the decisions we made and make the best of them. I think perhaps yours was a wiser choice than mine. Goodbye, my dear. I hope our next meeting will be for a frivolous and enjoyable purpose."

"I fear not, Dr. Walters. Stephen has challenged Edward Riley to a duel."

\*\*\*\*\*\*

# MASQUERADE

Stephen could not be turned aside from his decision and Lord Tilton could not dissuade Edward Riley from his. Julia was distraught. Either her husband or the man she loved could die in a duel. The men had decided on pistols as the weapon of choice. Newspapers now highlighted the event in every issue, making a stand-down by either party impossible. Stephen's gratification at Dr. Walters' report could not dissuade him. He knew Julia loved Edward, and that was reason enough to destroy him. The note from the old woman at the Maltby mansion was not encouraging: "Julia, stop Stephen's participation in the duel! I have a plan." But Lady Maltby, bright, witty and determined was not infallible. The Langley's prized ticking clock reminded Julia that a time of disaster was drawing near. She knew she could not allow either man to die.

******

The sun shone brightly through the windows of the Langley residence. It would shine even more brightly on the vast expanse that was Hyde Park. Stephen had made sure no magistrates would interfere. He was free to kill his wife's lover. His coat and trousers were freshly cleaned, his boots were immaculate. Julia received word that hundreds had assembled to see the duel. Stephen, proud and determined to trump his enemy, was about to descend the steps of his residence. Dozens waited on either side of the street to see his departure in the Langley barouche. As he began his descent, his right boot turned on a rock and he fell headlong onto the walk, but maintained enough composure to put his hands to his face to shield them from harm. The sidewalk crowd in shock and dismay shouted offers of help, but the Langley butler and footman were quick to lift him and bring him into the house. Not five minutes later the carriage carrying Dr. Walters came bounding down the street, and the physician made a quick exit from it and entry into the house. Amidst Stephen's wailing "I am disgraced! I am disgraced!" the doctor treated his wounds — cuts and scrapes to his arms and a sprained ankle.

"At least it's not broken and you've avoided a greater disaster," the doctor said an hour later.

# MASQUERADE

"Carry me to Hyde Park. I must fight!"

"You'll do no such thing," declared Dr. Walters. "Your opponent has been informed of your mishap and declares he will not fight a wounded man."

Julia, wringing her hands, but silent, had never seen Stephen cry, but he was crying now, lying immobile and distraught on the drawing room sofa.

"Leave me, leave me to my misery!" he shouted.

One by one, blanch-faced, the household staff hovering nearby moved off to go about their duties.

Dr. Walters motioned Julia away. "He'll recover soon in body, mind and spirit."

"Thank you for coming so quickly, Dr. Walters."

"You gave me plenty of time, dear Julia. The footman who came to fetch me arrived at 11:40, a full five minutes before Stephen's fall. Have you removed the rock from the step? I would hate to return for an encore presentation."

# CHAPTER TWENTY-FIVE

Lady Maltby leaned back in her chair at the mansion. "The investigation is well under way, Julia. Stephen's attorneys have tried to pry my identity from the informants I retain, but my retainers are large and I doubt they are prepared to match them, and any attempt to do so would be in vain. Even my informants are not aware of my identity. Of course, should these attorneys trace my roots to Paris, and further to my darling who publishes my books, my identity may be guessed, should these gentlemen of the law believe the dead write novels. All their efforts at revelation and recompense will be futile. English law is not applicable in France, anyway, to which I shall shortly return. My darling can hardly wait. So Stephen's efforts to determine the source of his anguish do not upset me. In fact, Julia, he will have cause to thank me as well as thank you, who insist upon it, for increasing his position and income, and erasing the nightmare of being number two son that haunts him. You shall have the man you love and he shall have what has eluded him all his life — self-respect and the power and adulation that comes with being a significant heir in our dramady. Stephen's bride-to-be is soon to arrive in London. The plot will not be left to chance."

"My pretended pregnancy has not fooled Stephen, and Dr. Walters' confirmation of his suspicion of the hoax has not forwarded the plot."

"It has done better. It has retained your virtue and reputation without destroying hope of achieving our goal. My previous novellas have not been followed to the letter, but satisfactory results have still been achieved. A divorce will occur because Stephen will request it. You will be doing him a favor."

## MASQUERADE

"But how?"

"Victor LeClair will arrive next week to do business with Stephen. A note to my darling Jacque about Stephen's financial brilliance has intrigued Leclair, a good Parisian friend, who is planning his retirement and has been unhappy with the financial advice offered him in Paris. Accompanying him will be his daughter Fleur. She has never been to London. You will show her our wonderful city. You will also host a dinner in honor of the extremely wealthy LeClairs and give Victor a chance to meet your impressive friends. The regal Earl of Tilton, Stephen's devoted client, accompanied by the brainy Amy Burton, always impresses, and Baron Willie and the Baroness always charm those they meet, and indicate the range of respect among the elite Stephen has garnered professionally and personally. Lady Brighton would also make a welcome addition to the group, indicating affection for family. The French respect the elderly. Please do not repeat to Margaret my reference to her age."

"Am I to propose this dinner to Stephen?"

"No need. He will request it of you. It is his way. Also include Mr. and Mrs. Cartwright, he, not only a client, but a member of Parliament, always impressive, and she a shrewd and observant wife. Stephen will not object to this addition. Cartwright has just come into a tidy sum as a result of the demise of an ancient relative, and is due another dinner as he contemplates how Stephen can help him invest it. The Cartwrights will be useful in forwarding our plot."

"This daughter — is she the young woman her parents are desperate to marry off?"

"She is indeed. You want Stephen to be happy. By relinquishing you he loses an angel, but gains greatly in other worldly, mercenary ways."

"You think Stephen will be attracted to her?"

"She is not a timid young woman. 'Aggressive' is a more accurate word."

"You're assuming a lot, Eugenia. Stephen patronizes married women. If his interest in them continues they cannot call a halt on threat of their husbands being informed of the affair."

"Monsieur Leclair will allow Stephen to believe Fleur is his young wife. Young wives, old husbands, easy game you know."

"Why would he do that?"

"Because I told him to. I told him that childless Stephen has a 'thing' about children. If they are not his he is affronted by them."

"And you believe Fleur will find my husband desirable."

"As I told you before, she finds most men desirable."

"She has no scruples, then, about cavorting with a married man."

"Actually, she has. That's her main redeeming feature. However, as you escort her about our city you will discreetly convey your unhappiness with your marriage, so she will know that she will not be injuring you by enjoying your husband, but rather forcing him to free you to marry her."

"Her father will allow this?"

"All her father will know is that Stephen has defiled his daughter. Only marrying her can put the matter right, and since this will meet with your approval, LeClair will have no pangs of conscience about defrauding you."

"And her mother?"

"I made sure she remains safely in Paris, attending to other matters. An emotional woman is best kept at home when promoting a business transaction. Her presence would only complicate things.

# MASQUERADE

Take Fleur on a London tour before the dinner. She must know of your disenchantment with Stephen before she meets him. She can then feel free to use her feminine wiles to have her way with him. Stephen's cuts and bruises are barely visible now, and his ankle has healed nicely. A new chapter begins."

"The story you have begun and the complications you envision are more than my mind can process."

"Julia, what are you complaining about? I've done all the hard work. All you have to do is follow the script. A nice cup of tea will settle your stomach and your mind."

"There is a limit to how much good that wonderful beverage can achieve."

Lady Maltby patted her hand and left for the kitchen, where a pot of hot tea awaited her. Upon her return Julia was more relaxed as her friend knew she would be.

Julia sipped the tea. This is delicious. "Whatever is in it?"

"A blend I created from all corners of the world, a complicated blend, but as you see complication in tea can lead to a satisfying cup of tea, so too can complication in a plot. Monsieur LeClair loves fish and chips and Fleur adores rich pastry. Have them on the menu. Finish your tea, dear. I omitted Earl Grey. Do you think I should add it to my next blend?"

******

The week flew by and Julia hastened to complete her household tasks and her charitable visits to those in hospital and those residing in the less elegant parts of London. When the stagecoach horses came to a halt at the London station Stephen and Julia were there to greet their guests and take them in their barouche to the posh hotel that was to be their home for the next two weeks. The men would spend most of that time dealing with LeClair's vast financial and property holdings while Julia would entertain Fleur, or so she thought. But Fleur had not come to London to be entertained.

"I want to meet people. London sites I've read about in books, and books satisfy my interest in them. A lively, throbbing metropolis like London exists because of its people," said Fleur, as she and Julia sipped tea at a cafe in the hotel.

"What kind of people interest you?"

"Men," said Fleur flatly.

Julia laughed, but briefly. Fleur was serious.

"Men in the company of London sites are fine." She pulled a list from her reticule. "My research," she explained. "Let's stroll Pall Mall and St James Streets and visit the coffee and chocolate houses along the way. Perhaps the clubs on our route will allow a French visitor a peek at them."

Julia looked at her in amazement. The area she had targeted was the enclave of businessmen.

"We can share a biscuit here and there, and drink half a cup of tea or coffee in each house. This will give us time to relax, chat, and look around the premises to see and be seen."

"A stroll in Hyde Park can do that with less negative effect on our figures or pocketbooks."

"Hyde Park strollers are likely to come in pairs. You don't mind strolling London streets, do you? It's excellent exercise, and more interesting than flowers and trees."

"Can't I tempt you with ANY historic sites?"

"You can — Parliament. We can sit upstairs and watch the proceedings. I've brought my opera glasses." She fished a pair out of her reticule.

"I don't know what they will be discussing today. The subject may bore you."

"The subject doesn't matter. We can visit the House of Lords today and the House of Commons another day."

"I don't know how many men there are unmarried or widowed," Julia said wryly.

"But you can find out, can't you, if I think they look interesting?"

But Lords was delayed for another day. After three hours of sampling coffee houses, Fleur with interest and Julia with embarrassment, a tired Julia persuaded an indefatigable Fleur to sit quietly in a sparsely filled coffee house, undistracted, and talk.

"You think I'm mad, don't you, Julia?"

"Not at all, I —"

"I would if I were you. But I'm me, and I'm desperate. I'm inflicting on you what my parents have inflicted on me, not a generous gift for your hostess." She sipped her tea, then pushed the cup away. "I'm an only child, well-educated and interested in men, but I don't feel the need to marry without love. My parents feel otherwise. They want a son-in-law, they want grandchildren, and they want an heir for their fortune. They don't like their male cousins and nephews and uncles. They know them too well, and they do have faults aplenty. There is no guarantee my husband won't have them either, but they'll have some choice in the matter, so they think, and he will at least be close family and the father of their grandchildren. I do complain a lot. I wonder where I got that from. I have other interests, ancient history and art. My parents fear I will be ancient history before they die, and my watercolors are a waste of time and useless in attracting a man, they say."

"I paint in watercolors, and my friend Amy Burton, who will soon marry Lord Tilton, is an expert in Greek and Roman art."

"Were your watercolors an influence in attracting your husband? Was your friend's knowledge germane to her winning Lord Tilton?"

"Probably not."

"Our interests intrigue and nurture us, but of what importance is that before marriage? Although I'm very interested in men, I don't have to marry one. I've had experiences my parents are unaware of that have given me great pleasure, intellectual or physical, but never both. I can continue this way. Money is an attraction that can keep me going into old age, should the good Lord grant me a long life. But while my parents are alive, and I love them dearly, I must do as they say. I am their heir whether I do or not. Other prospects have been dismissed. But when they pass I would live with the guilt of not having been a dutiful daughter, and though they are both in good health, the years are passing and one never knows. Have I shocked you?"

"You have enlightened me. You have great trust on a short acquaintance."

"I read character well. That makes me hard to please. You must have a happy marriage to be so serene and understanding."

"Perhaps 'resigned' would be the better word. We had better go. Stephen gave your father tickets to Covent Garden tonight and you will need time to dress."

Fleur put her hand on Julia's as she attempted to rise. "No, I have plenty of time. What do you mean 'resigned.'?"

"I should not have said that. It is a private matter."

"I have shared a private matter with you, and I assure you I will not reveal a private matter you reveal to me."

"Stephen is a good man and has provided well for me."

## MASQUERADE

"But you have no children. He can't have them," Fleur declared flatly.

"I'm sure he can. I don't want any — with him."

"Other women," Fleur said softly. "But why? You're so lovely, so gracious. Has he explained the cause of his behavior?"

"He denies it. He finds no fault with me except that I keep him childless."

"He's got a title, but no inheritance to go with it, I've heard. Resentment often seeks an outlet. Can you still feel some affection for him?"

"I lead a cosmopolitan life. I'm grateful to him for that."

"Surely other men have admired you. Has he not been jealous?"

"Jealous? Yes, very, but not jealous enough to give me a divorce."

Fleur was thunderstruck. "You'd go that far?"

"If I could."

Fleur was silent, then, "but a woman can't."

They paid and left the premises. A horse trotting briskly down the street sprayed dirt a mere two feet from where they stood. "A cosmopolitan life," echoed Fleur. They both laughed and whisked the dirt off the hems of their dresses.

******

"A masquerade ball, how exciting!" said Fleur. "I look forward to your dinner, I have clothes circumspect enough for that, but a masquerade ball days after — I shall want a gown more special than what I've brought."

"Have you no special gowns?"

"Tons that my parents have not seen, but most suitable for the exciting escapades I enjoy from time to time. My parents examined my wardrobe before we left Paris, as I knew they would, and the conservative garments I brought met with their approval. I want a smashing gown for the masquerade ball and several more to take home for future use."

"You anticipate future use? You do not expect to achieve your goal in London?"

"I am a romantic and a dreamer, Julia, but I am also a realist."

"Perhaps with your purchases we can link all three without a 'but also.'"

"You are very optimistic for a 'resigned' woman."

"And you are very energetic and tireless in pursuit of a dream. You've given me hope. Our first stop on today's pilgrimage will be Willie's on Fleet Street. You will meet Lord Wllie and Georgina, my best friend, at our dinner. Should his fabrics not satisfy, we will move on to Draper's and more until you have the fabrics you desire.

"At each stop Fleur acquired fabrics for future use, but it was five shops later that she found the longed-for fabric for the masquerade ball and a modiste with the spirit of adventure and the talent to realize the conception Fleur imagined for it. A dress of pale blue satin with folds of white satin at the scooped-out bosom, with a bit of white mechlin lace crushed above it. The sleeves were short and of mechlin lace as well, and the scarf was of white French silk. A rose clasp of carved mother-of-pearl at the cleavage was large enough to call attention to the breasts it separated, but not large enough to detract attention from them. White satin slippers with mother-of-pearl rosettes to match those at her bosom graced her feet and French kid gloves and a mechlin lace fan with ivory supports completed the ensemble.

Julia looked with awe at the reconstituted Fleur LeClair. "I don't see how any unmarried man could resist you," she told her charge. "But your father may protest the deep scoop above your breasts and the transparent mechlin lace which barely conceals what lies beneath it."

"He may protest all he likes." She swung the white French silk scarf about her shoulders. "He will see me encased in a scarf until we're at the ball."

"You will make many female enemies looking as you do. Only men will connive to talk to you, if they dare."

"Correct, and to the purpose. I have no desire to converse with women. That would be a total waste of time. They haven't been out in the world and can have little of interest to me to talk about."

"Shall you henceforth be silent with me as well?"

Fleur touched her hand. "No, Julia, not with you. I generalize."

She selected material for other gowns, one "to be designed conservatively should this London trip lead to the success I desire."

They left the shop, hailed a carriage, and were transported back, laughing and chatting with pent-up energy, to their respective abodes.

******

With a dinner party in the offing the next day Julia rushed to complete preparations for it, to consult with Mrs. North about additions to the menu, and to inquire of Reggie whether the barouche horses were in order to transport the LeClairs back to their hotel at the end of the festivities. The next morning, after rising early, she took a stroll of several blocks to Mrs. Compton to commiserate with her on the renewal of her gout and to bring her a new ointment she had procured from the apothecary to relieve the pain. After a twenty-minute visit she returned home just as dear Georgina struck the knocker on the front door.

"Georgina! Just in time for my first breakfast and your second."

Enjoying biscuits and hot chocolate, they compared notes. Georgina was wide-eyed at revelations about Fleur which could be shared, and Julia sat silent and thoughtful upon hearing the latest of how London was reacting to the accusations about the lord and lady of the house. Few thought the accusations against Lord Langley were fictitious and few believed the immorality of Lady Langley was accurate. "A London Lady has gone too far" was the cry of most women who had read the work. Lady Maltby had, of course, decided that Julia was not to wear Georgina's maternity frocks. News of Dr. Walters' visit and verdict had spread quickly. No one would believe the pretense of pregnancy.

"I can't inflict Stephen on Fleur," said Julia as they sipped and chatted.

"But you've made her aware of his weakness. If she chooses him you are not to blame."

"She may not choose him," said Julia, "and if she does not all our conniving will have been in vain."

"But you will have done your best to achieve your dream. And if she does choose him it will not be your doing. She has been warned."

"If Fleur looks elsewhere I will go on as before."

"If you must. You know your friends will lighten your burden any way they can."

While this dispiriting conversation was in progress Jameson delivered a message to Julia on a tray. It was from Lady Brighton.

## MASQUERADE

"Bless Aunt Margaret!" she said. She passed the note to Georgina, it read: "Success! Mrs. Williams has decided to make herself unavailable to Stephen with no replacement necessary."

"You see! Our efforts will not have been unrewarded. You will have success of some sort, even if not in its entirety."

"There are wives galore in London. With his looks, title and charm, he can have his pick."

"Lord Kendall is determined to have you, so take heart. Does Stephen think well of his potential father-in-law?"

"Stephen is besides himself with joy. LeClair is ecstatic about the financial plans for his estate."

"Surely he's conveyed his feelings about Stephen to Fleur."

"Perhaps. It's too late to turn back. I must see this drama through to its end."

"Expect a happy one, Julia. Negative expectations can abort the best-laid plans."

# CHAPTER TWENTY-SIX

Julia dressed smartly but simply. Her guests would honor the Langley name and household with more elegant attire, and she did not intend to out-dress her guests. Georgina and Robert were the first to arrive, Georgina laughing and jolly as always away from household tasks. The regal Lord Tilton arrived soon after with Amy Burton, Amy subdued but with the bright twinkle in her eye that Lord Tilton adored. Mr. and Mrs. Cartwright's greetings were respectful and reserved, though this was their second visit to the Langley residence and the member of Parliament and his wife had met most of the guests before. This was the effect aristocrats often had on the merely important. The LeClairs arrived last, and Stephen's effusive greeting reflected his gratitude at their presence. Fleur was silent, looking around her attractive, well maintained surroundings. All were ushered into the drawing room for a chat and refreshments while the dining room table, replete with flowers, was garnished with plates and tureens galore, silverware, napkins and mirror-perfect glassware. Julia had seated Fleur next to Stephen, who sat at the head of the table, and Fleur's father, or wife as Stephen supposed, opposite her. Stephen was therefore closest to pour her the soup she desired and cut the beef she chose as her first entree. Lord Tilton, on the other side of her, was doing the same for his Amy. As the meal progressed to jello and more elaborate desserts, Lord Tilton rose with a toast to the evening's hosts. Fleur rose with the rest, but briefly turned her back to the table. Monsieur LeClaire uttered a sharp intake of breath. He motioned to Fleur, but she seemed not to understand what he was trying to communicate. Georgina and Amy nearest her, could barely restrain giggles, but

# MASQUERADE

Mrs. Cartwright, closer to Julia, declared loudly, "Your lace has slipped."

"Oh, my," exclaimed Fleur, and her face reddened as she stood, turned her back to the table and attempted to adjust it. When she sat, no one but Monsieur LeClaire could refrain from laughter. The lace sat cockeyed above her breasts.

"Oh, nasty lace!" she declared as she whipped it off and placed it on her lap. The impenetrable lace had given way to a very penetrable view of what it had concealed, but Fleur continued chatting with Stephen as though nothing was amiss. Julia kept her eyes on Stephen, who was making a valiant effort to keep his eyes glued to Fleur's, but they often slipped, as how could they not, to his seat-mate's ample bosom. Monsieur LeClaire called in desperation across the table to his hostess, and Julia rose and walked to his daughter.

"Come with me. I have some lace that will not be reluctant to behave." And with an "Excuse me" Fleur followed her hostess who led her upstairs. Julia's bedchamber was all pastel and ruffles. Fleur looked in awe and said, "This is dreamland! You must sleep well." Julia smiled and opened the bottom drawer of the chest alongside her bed. A roll of lace lay curled in the midst of it, next to a sketch of a handsome man with curly black hair. Julia removed the lace and quickly closed the drawer.

"Your brother?"

"No, a friend. Now let me adjust this lace properly so it will cause you no more grief this evening."

"My drawings sit in drawers, too, Julia. Since men do not care for them or my conversation I am ill equipped to secure one. You are fortunate to have a husband who is at least interested in matters other than finance, law and politics. My chatter about antiquity seemed to intrigue him."

This was news to Julia. She surmised that the intrigue was about what lay lower than her face. When they returned to the dining room, Stephen's almost imperceptible nod indicated the women were to adjourn to the drawing room while the men continued with conversation and drink. But Lord Tilton, eager for more time with Amy, intercepted the nod and declared, "Stephen, tonight let's stay with the women and play charades."

"Changing syllables into words is too much for my head tonight, Gerald. Your intellect never wanes."

"We do it differently in France now, Stephen," said LeClaire. "We act out an object, person or message."

The women jumped at this opportunity to play-act, and Stephen was outvoted. All repaired to the drawing room for Charades. Georgina performed a suit she had seen in her favorite women's magazine, Only the women guessed it. Husband Robert performed the barouche he had recently bought, Victor imitated Napoleon, Fleur, Sarah Bernhardt, Mr. Cartwright the Ten of Clubs and Mrs. Cartwright a prostitute. No one guessed her imitation and the others looked uneasy when she revealed her choice. Julia was about to perform when Georgina suddenly rose, tipping Stephen's glass of white wine into the lap of Fleur LeClaire. Stephen quickly grabbed a napkin and began to blot the liquid dry, then stopped suddenly, flustered, not knowing how to proceed, Fleur calmly took the napkin from his hand and blotted the liquid herself...

"The color is a blend," she declared. "My lower half is now quite intoxicated."

Julia rose, the last to perform, beckoning Georgina to follow her.

"Did you do that on purpose, Georgina?"

"No, honestly, Julia. You know how clumsy I can be." She blushed. "But it was fortuitous."

## MASQUERADE

"It certainly was. Awareness of Fleur's body should now be firmly planted in Stephen's mind."

As the laughter and camaraderie continued, Julia repaired with Georgina to the library for her mandolin. She played a bittersweet song, and in her sweet voice sang it. She finished and all were silent.

Finally, Amy sighed in satisfaction. "That was lovely, Julia."

Julia took a cream tart from the tray Marie was passing around and asked, "Well, What playwright's words are reflected in this song?"

Her guests scrambled to guess. "I've got it," shouted Mrs. Cartwright, but she was wrong. The romantic message wrapped in the songwriter's choice was not the poet Blake's.

"We give up!" said Georgina.

Julia caressed the mandolin on her lap and said — "If music be the food of love, play on. Let me have excess of it — William Shakespeare."

So the evening ended on a thoughtful musical note. Amy and Gerald were the last to leave. As Gerald turned to Stephen with parting words about a business matter, Amy turned to Julia and said, "So true, my friend. So very true. Shakespeare also said, 'All the world's a stage and all the men and women merely players. They have their exits and their entrances.' So we'll be on our way. The play is barely half over."

******

The next day's mail brought a letter from brother Jonathan. He and their parents were well and anxiously awaiting her and Stephen's arrival for Christmas. About his future a decision was in the offing.

"I've found two adjacent properties that would make a grand estate, and a lovely lady ideal to go with them. I shall soon be as settled as you and Stephen, and glad of it."

"How little we are able to read each other's hearts," thought Julia," but he means he is happy, and the meaning is what matters."

The December Masquerade Ball was in three days, before which she and Fleur would concern themselves with the serious business of Parliament. Julia had a list of all members in each House, with a check mark indicating those of marital availability. The two women learned a lot about the pros and cons of the new tax proposal, the need for more financial support for the indigent, and the housing problem created by the influx of people from the Continent. The main speakers were either ineligible or unappealing as marriage material. There were a number of unmarried or widowed men in both chambers, but Fleur dismissed them. "I have no interest in a man who cannot speak," she said.

# CHAPTER TWENTY-SEVEN

London buzzed with anticipation of The Masquerade Ball. It was sponsored by the Duchess of Marmaduke, the eccentric widow of the even more eccentric Duke. She had a propensity for wearing odd garments and doing odd things. If the day was cloudy and she wished for the sun, she dressed for the sun. If she felt like dancing upon returning from a dance recital, her carriage would lurch to a stop, and she would leap from the vehicle to the horror of onlookers, and dance with the first person she met. She exercised daily, was as healthy as the proverbial horse, and was never injured or arrested for her outlandish behavior. Rather, her lines and wrinkles spared her from disgrace or even laughter. Awe was the usual reaction to her antics. At the ball there would be dancing, but no official entertainment. Singers, acrobatics, magic acts? None. The guests would provide the entertainment. What this meant was only to be discovered at the ball. The guests had been invited to dress as they wished with no notice of the season, but a mask of some sort had to be in evidence, in the hand or on the person of each guest. Only the wealthy could afford the Marmaduke Masquerade, and Julia felt privileged to be one of them.

Stephen looked with admiration as his wife descended the stairs. "You look lovely, my dear, just lovely." Julia was a vision in white chiffon. She held a gold and black mask in her right hand. A gold Byzantine medallion graced the center of her bosom, a match to the thin, gold Byzantine band that encircled her head and sprouted three white feathers. Her white kid gloves held a black lace fan, and her gold tapestry slippers were firmly planted on the landing. Stephen put a gold tapestry wrap around her shoulders and they left the house, hastening in the cool December air to enter the barouche in which Reggie would take them to a night of revelry and mystery. They were early in order to witness the guests as they entered, instead of bustling through crowds to see who was there and what they were wearing. Georgina and Robert and Amy and Gerald had already arrived with the same intent. Julia's friends were in yellow and orange with matching masks. "Yellow is so happy," exclaimed Georgina, and "Orange is so fall. It's not winter yet!" exclaimed Amy. Most of the men wore black or white evening attire, a suitable background and no distraction to their stylish ladies fair. The musicians, elevated at the front of the ballroom, were greeting guests with the ebullient Baroque music of William Boyce, while the Duchess of Marmaduke welcomed them personally at the door. The ballroom exuded festivity, from the flowers and trees aglitter with candles to the shimmering crystals on the gaslit chandeliers and the sideboards in bright red cloth holding the delectable food and drink invitingly displayed upon them. The ceiling featured dozens of multi-colored scoops of cloth around the chandeliers, and laughter and chatter was rapidly filling the ballroom with the entry of an avalanche of guests. The men were active in greeting and chatting with those they knew from business or their clubs, while Julia and her friends watched and admired the incoming crowd.

"There's Jack Frost. Rather stiff. Is he on stilts?" asked Georgina.

"He can't walk otherwise," explained Julia. That's Lord Mackintosh. Gout."

"Oh, that snowman and his wife. I wouldn't dare be seen as a snow-woman, even at a masquerade ball," exclaimed Georgina.

The men had just rejoined their ladies.

"That grand old tree is rightly accompanied by a rose bush," noted Lord Tilton.

## MASQUERADE

"Oh, what kind of beast is that, all brown and black and crusty?" asked Robert.

"There has to be a killjoy on parade even at an elegant ball," noted Amy. "Not an indication, I hope, of things to come."

It was now that they looked at the cards the Duchess had extended to them along with her greeting. Thy were dance cards.

"For married women?" exclaimed Georgina.

"A twist on the usual dance cards for unmarried women, but hardly for singles," noted Amy. "I see few of those here."

"The instructions say you can't dance with your wife or your intended," said Lord Tilton. "That's most unfair!"

"But exciting," noted Amy.

"Wives will be careful to note whom their husbands choose," said Georgina.

"And husbands who select their wives," added Julia. "Ah, there's the Duchess about to sit and watch the proceedings. Let's inquire what the mischievous old dear has in mind for this evening."

The men declined to inquire. Their women would tell them. Amy and Georgina followed Julia to their seated hostess.

"My dears, no food, no drink?"

"We prefer to chat with you, dear lady. What has the Duchess of Marmaduke wrought?"

"Scavenger hunts, promenades and a surprise. Each dance will be short. No country reels here. Twenty minutes cavorting in a group allows little chance to meet new people and have an adventure."

"Adventure, Duchess? It sounds a bit frightening."

"Not at all, Lady Willie, but more than a bit amusing."

Victor and Fleur LeClaire had just entered, and the women, after thanking the Duchess, hastened to greet them and further explain the dance cards and instructions the Duchess had left for latecomers at the door. Fleur's shawl was tightly wrapped across her bosom, giving her father no indication of the sight beneath. The dance music was now beginning. As the tables began to be depleted of hardy liquid and anxious patrons awaited delivery of more, the dances became less sedate in response to the tempo and the beverages that had been consumed. Gavottes were followed by minuets and several quadrilles, and the intoxicating refreshments had to be replaced with more rapidity. A signal from the Duchess indicated the master of ceremonies was now to announce a scavenger hunt. A gold pin would be awarded to any lady able to wrest s blue cravat from any man, no help from the man allowed. Several dances later another scavenger hunt was announced. A white flower, real or fake, was to be retrieved by a man from a woman's garment, the prize, the flower. And on it went. A blue feather, a bit of white lace, an embroidered male handkerchief, a silver female slipper. Julia pulled Georgina and Amy aside.

"Something strange is afoot. The hunt has become particularized on items worn by Fleur and Stephen."

"Indeed. And Stephen has rescued Fleur from men who accosted her for her pearl broach and torn the mechlin lace from her bodice. Her father is bewildered and growing angry," said Georgina.

"I see Eugenia's hand in this," said Amy.

Their eyes turned to the Duchess of Marmaduke, who now sat chatting with another woman, fully masked and dressed in glittering grey. As the hubbub died down after the latest infringement on their persons, the guests were brought to attention as the musicians broke into a royal march. Entering the ballroom was a very late and very elegant man. His attire, a tightfitting ensemble of white and gold was a match to Julia's. His gold and black mask covered the upper part of his face, like hers, but his figure, curly hair and full lips proclaimed him a handsome man. Had a prince from the Continent stepped into the ballroom? He glanced quickly at his hostess and then walked purposefully toward Julia.

"The next dance is mine," he said.

Julia looked at her dance card. Her next partner was to be a "Match." Someone, she had thought, had surely written that in jest. He took her hand and led her to the dance floor as the musicians broke into a waltz. Considering what the revelers had witnessed and participated in thus far this dance seemed as appropriate as any. The couple danced as though they were one and were the cynosure of all eyes. The next dance was a waltz as well, and a short, fat man who held up his card and declared "I'm next," did so weakly.

'After this, sir, if you will allow me," said the mystery figure, and commenced the next waltz with Julia without waiting for the allowance. The two danced with no regard for their feet or where they were going. They had eyes only for each other. Fleur, standing with her father, remembered the drawing in Julia's cabinet drawer. The mask could not disguise that it was the same man.

"She's in love with him," she said softly to herself.

The question of his identity spread quickly. The woman in resplendent grey, still by Duchess Marmaduke's side turned to respond to a query from a member of the ton, who quickly passed the revelation on to those in his path to the table laden with fresh whisky and spirits. When this gallant's identity reached the ears of Georgina and Amy, it was no surprise. They had guessed as much. It was young Lord Kendall, heir and now master of the vast Marquis of Kendall's estates. They gave each other knowing looks and their eyes then went to the lady in grey.

"Stephen looks livid. Good heavens, what will he do?" wailed Georgina.

At the dance's conclusion, Stephen left Lord Wexler, his Club confrere, and hurried to confront Lord Kendall. "Leave this instant!" he commanded.

"I only came to waltz with your fair wife and for this." And he grabbed Julia to his breast and kissed her passionately on the lips.

Lord Langley's hands went for Edward's throat, but the interloper had quickly turned and hurried down the line spectators had hastily parted for him as he moved rapidly toward the door and made his exit.

Lord Langley turned toward his wife, his face a crimson fury which spoke the words his lips dared not utter. All he felt secure enough to say was "So you allow this?" He brushed past his wife and groups that were in his way as he made a beeline for Fleur and escorted her to the dance floor. A waiting woman and man who were obviously to be the next partners of the pair shrugged their shoulders and fell into each other's arms instead for the next waltz.

Georgina was now at Julia's side. "It's over dear. Calm yourself. Who could have known?"

A few feet away Amy and Gerald looked with compassion on an unsteady Julia.

Gerald nodded. "Yes, praise the Lord, it's over."

"Over? It's just beginning," responded Amy. "Stephen will have his revenge. He will keep his Julia and do the very thing she detests the most."

Georgina was hurried away for a dance. The need to release her pent-up emotion overcame the lady, and as her arm swung out in time to the music it slammed into the body of a short gentleman who lost his balance and his toupee and slid across the dance floor on his knees, stopping at the foot of a very large woman with a very large mouth.

"Are you proposing marriage?" she boomed.

The laughter bounced off the wall and echoed through the ballroom.

As the waltz was ending canopies of fabric floated to the floor, enveloping those beneath it who struggled to escape its folds, touching more than the fabric in their scramble to escape. Fleur and Stephen were under this first fabric collapse. There were more to follow.

"What a night," observed Amy, "and it's barely half over!"

The Duchess now signaled for a promenade. Walking and talking was the thing. There was so much to chat about.

# CHAPTER TWENTY-EIGHT

The only sound to be heard in the Langley carriage were the horses' hooves on the cobblestone streets. Lord Langley helped his wife alight, walked with her silently to their door, opened it and closed it behind them.

"Let me make one thing clear, Julia. You are my wife, you will remain my wife, and you will bear me children."

Her response was to hurry up the stairs, enter her bedchamber and lock the door. She spent the next half hour sobbing and shaking in the chair near her bed.

Stephen did not appear at breakfast or at dinner. The servants said that while she was in high morning conclave with Georgina and Amy he had come and gone within the space of ten minutes carrying several items of clothing. Distraught and comforted by her friends and servants for two days, she saw him on the third day as she was exiting the library. He kissed her on the cheek, inquired about the evening menu and behaved as if nothing was or ever had been amiss. She continued with the false facade, puzzled and uneasy until a note arrived from Amy. it was brief and to the point: "Stephen spent the last two nights with Fleur LeClair." Now Stephen's message was clear. She would be his forever and he would make no effort to dispense with other women who might strike his fancy. This would be her punishment for her betrayal and embarrassment of his eminent self. And what was to be his punishment for disrespecting his marriage vows? Apparently, nothing. What power did she have to punish? But she didn't want to punish. She wanted to exit his life. As she put the succinct but powerful message in her reticule, she saw there was an additional message on the back. "You are not alone, Julia. There is power in truth and the certainty of release. Take heart."

\*\*\*\*\*\*

The following day Stephen was surprised by a visit from Victor LeClair who was two hours early for an appointment to discuss purchase of the Maltby estate. Stephen rose to shake LeClair's hand, but met with no physical response.

"Take a good look at your cherished office, Lord Langley. You will soon be begging for handouts in the street and huddling in doorways for warmth. You have deflowered my daughter and I will destroy you."

"I've done no such thing! What daughter?"

"Fleur, you fool! How dare you violate my precious virgin prize, the light of my life, the hope of my old age!"

"Your daughter! But you said she was your wife."

"Violating my wife would be acceptable you varlet, you thief?"

"She's lying, I did no such thing. She's shown an interest in me. I believe she wants me to divorce my wife and marry her and this is her way of achieving it."

"My daughter didn't tell me you'd been sleeping with her. How dare you impugn her character. I was informed by the servants at the hotel. While I sleep innocently two doors away you are deflowering my Fleur. My power is sure and my influence is vast. I will reduce you and your world to ruble. It is my will. My wife will think even this is not enough!"

"If Fleur were willing —"

"My daughter will not be willing. What tricks, what smooth, clever words have you used to embroil my child in your lustful action I do not know, but you will pay a heavy price for what you have done. Who will have her now? She is damaged merchandise. You have deprived her of a worthy husband and children and me and my wife of grandchildren and a male heir. She's my only child and all I have is hers, and the Le Clair line and fortune dies with her. You are a beast beyond belief and you shall suffer!"

"Wait! Is there nothing I can do to make amends? I'll serve your business needs without cost. The Maltby estate shall be yours without any payment to me. The other business ventures we've discussed — no charge for any of them. I can be valuable to you."

"You expect me to put a price on my daughter's virginity? I say again, look around at what you're losing. In two days I leave with my daughter's virginity as intact as it can be after your pilfering. Your moral disgrace will bring your house down, which is the least you deserve." Victor LeClair turned to leave.

"Wait, Monsieur LeClair! Have you spoken to Fleur about this?"

"She is in tears and speechless."

"If Fleur will take me as husband I will marry her."

Now LeClair was speechless. Then, "But what of your wife?"

"She doesn't love me."

"She doesn't love me, she doesn't understand me," mimicked LeClair. Then — "Lord Kendall, is it?"

Stephen nodded.

LeClair was silent for a moment. "Can you love my girl?"

"I can. She's bright and — appealing."

"Humph," grunted LeClair. "I'll speak to her, see if she'll have you,"

"Thank you, sir. You won't regret it, she won't regret it."

He grunted again. "We'll see."

As LeClair left the Langley office his mind was whirling with plans. A financial genius to manage the LeClair's extensive holdings, a son, a husband for Fleur at last. He need not explain to his wife the circumstances surrounding the engagement. But Fleur must like him enough to agree. He walked out into the sunshine and deeply inhaled the fresh air. "Two nights of passion," he muttered, then laughed. "Oh, these young people!"

******

The LeClairs delayed their departure for Paris. There was much to be done — the special license, Church of England approval of divorce, Parliamentary approval, the banns and settling the purchase of the Maltby estate, at which Fleur and her husband would live for part of the year. There were the LeClair estates in France to manage as well as new ventures to increase LeClair's retirement income in the years ahead.

# CHAPTER TWENTY-NINE

Happy were the newly married Lord and Lady Tilton when the banns were announced for their friends Julia and Edward and Stephen and Fleur. They held a prenuptial celebration for the couples in the ballroom of the Tilton mansion, an intimate affair for two hundred friends and well-wishers. Now that all was resolved between them Edward was willing to amicably greet his former foe, but Stephen would only go so far as to nod his acknowledgement of Edward's presence.

"He'll soften in time," said Fleur.

Mrs. LeClair's presence evinced a flurry of good cheer as she made her way about the ballroom. She was a lovely lady, smiling, soft-spoken and kind. Mrs. Cartwright was an especially treasured guest. She had pushed her reluctant husband Willard not only to approve Julia and Stephen's divorce, but to expedite its approval by the House of Commons. She had also successfully gotten him to persuade Mr. \_\_\_\_, a Whig, not a Tory like himself, to do likewise, despite his wife's prodding that he do no such thing. Mrs. Cartwright deduced that Mrs. \_\_\_\_ had been one of Stephen's night-time adventures. And indeed, she was yet another woman Lady Brighton had threatened with exposure if she did not relinquish her hold on Stephen, which she reluctantly did. It was noted by many that Mrs. Jacque Duprê bore a striking resemblance to the late Lady Maltby, who had passed on seven years earlier. Small world. Julia took Mrs. Cartwright aside to offer her profuse thanks for her assistance.

"I saw Stephen eyeing you at our dinner party. He didn't intrigue you?"

# MASQUERADE

"Not at first, but he did after I met him countless times at his office. He had insisted I accompany Willard to hear his financial proposals, most unusual for a banker. What intrigued me was why he persisted, his intent was obvious to me but not to my husband, when he had such a lovely wife to give him pleasure. He finally made me an offer I refused. I assured him, as he wished, that I would not divulge its contents to Willard."

"He's handsome, he can be charming when he wishes. So you weren't captivated?"

"Good heavens, no. He's as boring as my Willard. I don't mind boring, and I would have considered him for dessert if I hadn't met you. I usually avoid sleeping with men whose wives I've met, especially ones I like, and I like you. Boring, you see, is familiar, comforting, but I like mine spiced with adventure. I'm the adventure for Willard, but I must find mine elsewhere. You, my dear, have done a remarkable thing. You've taken daring action to achieve the man you love and you've done it in a moral way. Love! What else is there to fill a woman's heart, to make her existence complete? She can never be a merchant, a banker, a member of Parliament to fill at least some of the void with an occupation that fills a worldly need. She can have children, that comes close, but only a man, the right man, can meet the need for love she was born to share. Again, congratulations! I admire you immensely."

"I could not have done it alone. Without A London Lady my story would end differently."

"I am fortunate A London Lady has not exposed my infidelity. I've been careful in preserving the privacy of my liaisons, but she is a shrewd one, with many resources. I live in constant fear she will light upon my affairs and cause havoc in my life."

"You have been so kind in your assistance to me that I shall put your mind at rest. She is leaving London and will no longer be reporting marital escapades in our city. She has fallen in love."

"My, my! Well, good luck to her — and good fortune to me." She gazed into the distance and her eyes held a wistful look. "Perhaps some day if Willard is gone and I'm still here I'll find it too. I won't be young, but love isn't beholden to youth for its appearance. It is for those of any age who have experienced something of the world and learned the nature and the value of love."

There was music to dance and sing to, and the musicians continued long into the night. Fleur was incandescent, delighting everyone with her appreciation of their presence. She took Julia and Georgina aside to further vent the explosive joy in her heart.

"Thank you so much for Stephen, Julia. I want so much to make him happy."

"I have no doubt you will."

"It was almost too late. I'm almost thirty, you know. But in Stephen, I met the man I'd hoped for, the man of my dreams." She gazed dreamily into the distance.

"A man of intelligence, organization and charm?" prompted Georgina.

Fleur's eyes gleamed. "A man with an enormous talent. I've never been so thoroughly plowed in all my life!"

Lord Tilton was fast approaching. "Julia, The Earl of Weston's new wife is standing alone with no one to talk to. She's a farmer's daughter."

"I'll go to her," exclaimed Fleur.

"But you've been a city girl all your life."

"That doesn't matter," explained Julia. "She has a great interest in plowing, planting and reaping."

Fleur laughed heartily before hurrying off.

"Poor child," said Lord Tilton. "She will soon have to cope with an unfaithful husband."

"On the contrary, Gerald. I think she will cure Stephen of his wanderlust."

"She is so intelligent, so gifted?"

"So persistent. Stephen is not likely to have energy left for anyone else."

The evening ended with multiple toasts to the happy couples, and some of the departing guests needed help in negotiating their way to the entry and to their carriages. Julia and Edward would wed at the little chapel near her parents' home. Then they would travel to Kendall Manor, Julia's new and Edward's ancestral home. Fleur and Stephen would wed in St. James Church, the venue justified by Stephen's rise to power and wealth. The father and brother he seldom saw would be heartily welcome to the wedding of the Langley who was heir to the LeClair estates and fortune. They would be happily introduced, and no doubt enchanted, by his French bride and her family.

Julia's friends would make the journey for her wedding, but the thought of what lay beyond with her absence was unsettling.

Lady Brighton hugged Julia. "You will always be my darling niece." She wiped away tears. "I will have another, but no one will replace you in my heart."

"Nor you in mine, Aunt Margaret. Our love and friendship will continue always."

"I'll miss you so!" wailed Georgina.

"Haven't you and Robert talked about buying a country estate to escape the summer heat of London? Edward tells me there is one for sale no more than half an hour from ours."

"When London suits you, come to us," said Amy. "Come however you like and whenever you like. The pleasure will be ours."

"If travel is in your future, and it certainly should be, visit us in Paris," said Eugenia. "Your presence will be a gratifying reminder that good things can happen to good people, with help from above and from determined friends who believe in happy endings."

THE END

www.ingramcontent.com/pod-product-compliance
Lightning Source LLC
LaVergne TN
LVHW010205070526
838199LV00062B/4508